Out the window

Clint rushed to the door, which was still swinging back and forth. Clint knew better than to charge right in after a desperate man, so he ducked to one side at the last second to press his back against the wall beside the door's frame.

The instant before his shoulder hit the wall, two shots punched fresh holes through the flimsy wood. Gritting his teeth and edging away from the door a step or two, Clint brought the Colt up and listened for any hint of his target.

For a moment, he could only hear the echo of gunfire. But then his ears picked out the traces of wood scraping against wood.

His man was opening a window, Clint decided. More than likely, the shooter already had one foot out and was about to drop onto the ground outside the boardinghouse.

Clint wasn't about to let the man get away that easily. Not after he'd been forced to abandon a perfectly good poker game to chase him.

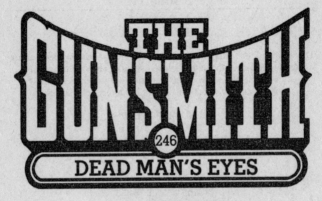

THE GUNSMITH

246

DEAD MAN'S EYES

J. R. ROBERTS

JOVE BOOKS, NEW YORK

This is a work of fiction. Names, characters, places, and incidents either are the product of the author's imagination or are used fictitiously, and any resemblance to actual persons, living or dead, business establishments, events, or locales is entirely coincidental.

DEAD MAN'S EYES

A Jove Book / published by arrangement with
the author

PRINTING HISTORY
Jove edition / June 2002

Visit our website at
www.penguinputnam.com

ISBN: 0-515-13312-4

A JOVE BOOK®
Jove Books are published by The Berkley Publishing Group,
a division of Penguin Putnam Inc.,
375 Hudson Street, New York, New York 10014.
JOVE and the "J" design
are trademarks belonging to Penguin Putnam Inc.

PRINTED IN THE UNITED STATES OF AMERICA

10 9 8 7 6 5 4 3 2 1

ONE

Clint Adams had been called The Gunsmith for so long that even he might have thought that he'd been born with that name. Dating back for more years than he could remember, the moniker had been hung around his neck like a permanent noose and he'd never been able to shake free of it. Not that he wanted to be rid of it so badly, but it would have been nice if more people knew him as just plain old Clint Adams.

In fact, that was exactly why he enjoyed staying around the town of Labyrinth in West Texas. Most of the folks that lived there had known him too long to think of him as The Gunsmith anymore. To them, he was Mr. Adams who'd come back to town after being away for a year or so and was now staying at the Lone Star Hotel. Those folks knew enough about Clint's colorful reputation as one of the best-known gunslingers alive, but they were able to look past that.

Clint enjoyed being somewhere where he could relax for a while. Somewhere where he could let his guard down and savor the simple pleasures in life like a drink with a friend or a fine summer day.

After all, a comfortable mattress beat the hell out of a

bedroll on the ground any day. And it was simple things like those that Clint enjoyed the most.

Clint thought about those simple things as he headed over to the town's livery and took his horse Eclipse out for a ride. The Darley Arabian stallion had always been fond of the open trail, but lately even he seemed content to stay in one spot.

As Clint rode him out of town and let the stallion run full speed, he wondered if Eclipse wasn't getting just a little wider beneath the saddle. Even if that were the case, Eclipse was still able to charge fast enough to turn the surrounding scenery into a rush of browns and greens while cutting through the air like a warm knife through butter.

When they circled back to the town's border, horse and rider were both enjoying racing across the open trail without a care in the world. More and more lately, Clint had been missing that feeling. That longing had been running just beneath Clint's surface for some time now.

No matter how much he enjoyed the quiet life, Clint knew that he wasn't meant to get more than a taste at any one time. He'd been staying close to home over the last few months. Despite a few distractions that pulled him away on account of one person or another needing his help, Clint had been more than content to remain a resident of Labyrinth.

But more and more lately, he'd started to feel something inside him breaking through like cracks forming in a frozen lake as springtime approached. His contentment was starting to break apart whenever he got even the slightest taste of the wandering that usually filled his life. And just like that same lake, Clint wasn't meant to remain motionless.

After settling Eclipse back into the livery, Clint had started to head for Rick's Place when something out of the corner of his eye caught his attention. It was a shape in one of the back corners of the stable that he'd all but forgotten about during the course of these recent months.

Clint turned away from the front door and headed toward that dark corner, where a rather large piece of his property lay beneath an old tarp. Before he could step up to it, however, Clint unlocked a fence made with wood and chicken wire, which served more as a nuisance to other curious customers than a genuine threat to anyone who might want to help themselves to what lay beyond it. His key fit into a rusty lock and the gate swung open on noisy hinges.

Smiling as he stepped up to the tarp and pulled it down, Clint looked upon his old wagon as though he was gazing through a window into his past. The wagon wasn't anything too special. Just a sturdy structure on four wheels that was small enough to be pulled by a single horse with a good back. Inside were all the tools of Clint's more respectable trade of repairing or even constructing firearms.

It was that wagon that had earned Clint his nickname. And it was that wagon that reminded him even more of traveling on the open trail without worrying about where he might wind up or how long he'd been away. Walking around the wagon, Clint ran his hands over the weathered planks and an occasional spot of chipped paint.

There were plenty of unfriendly memories attached to the vehicle as well. Most recently, a crazy man had tried to write himself into The Gunsmith's legend by stealing the wagon as well as Clint's identity for his own. But such memories were only a few unfortunate shadows, easily outnumbered by years of good times spent riding across the country.

"That's funny," said a voice from behind Clint. "I never pegged you for the sentimental type."

Clint didn't bother turning around right away. He'd heard the other man's footsteps against the loose straw on the floor the moment he'd entered. And now that he heard the man speak, he knew exactly who it was. With his hand still resting on the side of the wagon, Clint replied, "I guess that just comes with old age."

Rick Hartman stepped through the open gate and started looking the wagon over himself. "Better not start talking like that. If you're old, then how the hell am I supposed to feel?"

Clint turned around to look at the man who'd been his friend for so many years. The saloon owner and gambler was just as much a fixture in Labyrinth as the place he ran, and was just as well known by folks for miles around. Shaking his head, Clint said, "Might as well feel just like I do."

"Which is?"

"Lately . . . every bit as beaten up as this old wagon. It's getting to be where I hate to look in the mirror anymore in case one of these times I see an old-timer staring straight back at me."

Hartman put on the grin that Clint was all too familiar with after such a long friendship. "Aw, don't give me that," he said. "I may not be the sharpest tool in the shed, but I ain't blind."

"What's that supposed to mean?"

"I've seen the look you've had on your face the last couple of times you came into my saloon, and it usually comes right before you disappear to help some fine-looking lady in trouble or take on some kind of problem that's not any of your business."

Clint started to protest, but couldn't get out more than half a word before he stopped himself. "Okay, Rick. If you're so smart, then maybe you can tell me what I'm thinking right now."

"Let's see." The saloon owner put a hand to his chin and surveyed the scene in front of him carefully. "I'd say that you're trying to come up with some excuse to pull out of town. You're probably thinking back to when you could travel without being recognized and wondering how long it's been since the last time you roamed without a care in the world."

"Damn," Clint said. "You're good."

TWO

Hartman nodded sagely for a second or two before he rolled his eyes. "Jesus, Clint you've only been here for a few months and you're already aching to get out again. I heard that stallion of yours thundering down the street and thought you might've found a reason to pack up right now. That's why I came over here so quick."

Opening the back of the wagon, Clint looked inside and ran his hands over the tools, which still hung in the exact spots where he'd left them. "The funny thing is that it felt so good to get back here after being away," he said. "And here I am, not even half a year later, and I want to leave again."

"What's wrong with that?"

"Shouldn't there be a time when a man sinks roots somewhere for a while?"

Hartman mulled that over for a bit. "You and Lily seem to be getting along well enough. She makes a decent living running the Lone Star Hotel, so I guess she could support you well enough. Sure," he said while slapping Clint on the shoulder. "You sink your roots. I'll bet Lily's even got a job for you as a cook or maybe a bellboy."

Clint let out a heavy sigh as he waited for the laughter

from his friend. He didn't have to wait long before Hartman busted out loud enough for his voice to echo within the stable's walls.

"You finished yet?" Clint asked once the other man seemed to get a grip on himself.

Hartman fought to suppress his grin and shrugged. "You're not just any man, Clint. Labyrinth isn't going anywhere and neither is Lily. Go stretch your legs for a bit and come back when it suits you. Lord knows you'll find something out there to keep you busy."

"That's just the point," Clint said. "Maybe I've spent too much time keeping busy and not enough investing in a future. I've seen firsthand what happens to men that live like there's no tomorrow. Especially the ones that take on the kind of life that I've got.

"They wind up flat on their backs inside a box beneath six feet of dirt. It doesn't matter how good you are, how fast, or how smart. Sooner or later, someone is going to be better or luckier than you and they'll take you out. I've dodged plenty of bullets with my name on them, Rick. Eventually, even my luck will run out."

Although they had been in the back of Clint's mind for some time, the words seemed especially powerful after they'd been let out in the open. Hearing them, Clint thought about all the times in the last year that he'd been shot at and lived to tell the tale. Sure, he'd caught more than a few bullets, and he had the scars to prove it. He bore them like grim reminders of just how close to the edge he'd chosen to live.

The more he watched Clint move around the wagon, the more Hartman started to show genuine concern on his face. "I've never known you to get so concerned about the past," he said. "And as for your luck, I've seen you play enough poker to know that you've got more luck than the rest of the men in this town put together."

"I can't argue that. But I've got a good life here. Maybe

I shouldn't be so anxious to throw it all away."

Now, Hartman looked deadly serious as he took hold of Clint's shoulder and spun him around to look him square in the eyes. "Listen to me and listen good. I've known you for a hell of a long time and you never came close to throwing your life away. Call it wisdom or just something that comes with bein' around for a while, but every man needs to take stock of his life now and then. That's what all of this is. Your only problem is that you have a hard time knowing how to deal with a regular life."

For a moment, Clint was surprised at Hartman's sudden change of attitude. But he listened to the man speak, and it didn't take long before his words started sinking in.

"I've got some news for you," Hartman continued. "We all wind up in that box you were talking about. It takes some longer than others, but every last one of us gets there eventually."

"I know that, Rick."

"Is that a fact? Because sometimes I wonder."

Clint turned to look at the old wagon, and then started walking toward the flimsy gate. After Hartman stepped outside as well, Clint locked up the fence and headed for the set of front doors. He lifted his face to the warmth of the sun and took a deep breath. "Maybe I do need to get away. Just for a little while."

"And what the hell do you think I've been trying to tell you?" Hartman asked with a sly grin.

"I guess a part of me thought I'd stick around here awhile longer. This place does feel like home. And I've even managed to go for a couple of weeks without someone coming in to take a shot at me."

"Don't give me that," Hartman said. "I've known you too long to hear that old line. You're too much of an old warhorse to be put to pasture this early. If you don't get some punk kid drawing down on you every so often, you start to feel neglected. Either that . . . or you get itchy waiting for that next shoe to drop."

That last part struck a nerve inside Clint that told him it could be nothing but the truth. "You know what bothers me the most about you?" Clint asked.

"I wouldn't know where to start."

"How about with the fact that you're right too damn much."

Hartman nodded and took a look at the sky himself. "You know something? I've always envied you. I'm just as much a part of this town as the ruts in the streets and don't mind it a bit. But every time you roll through here, I know you've been roaming from one end of the map to another and I can't help but feel envious."

"The grass is always greener, huh?"

"Something like that."

"Well, before you kick me out of your town, how about I buy you a drink? One old man to another."

THREE

As the day wore on and the sun made its rounds across the sky, Labyrinth went through surges of life similar to any living thing. At certain times, the town seemed to just lie on its back without making a move. But at other times, it rattled with energy that flowed through its streets like fresh blood through veins.

Once the summer heat began to fade away with the arrival of night, Labyrinth stretched out and woke up as the people inside its boundaries poked their heads out of work and home to gather and swap the news of their day. The late coaches rumbled into town from every direction, forcing streams of people to jump out of their way while crossing from one boardwalk to another.

As the sun shrank down to a golden sliver on the horizon and the shadows leaked out to cover the faces of every building, more faces could be seen and more voices could be heard. It was at night when the town really came to life. No sooner had the daylight been swallowed up completely than it was replaced by the flickering illumination of lanterns burning along the side of the street; the flames dancing in time to the music of pianos being played at the local saloons.

Most of the people out and about at that time of night walked in small groups to or from those saloons. Some were in search of a better place to eat or simply a different room in which to drink. Others made their way to a new kind of entertainment to be found in a nearby gambling hall or whorehouse.

There were also those people who were content to stay outside and drink in the cooling air as it blew lazily through Labyrinth. Two of those kind were standing outside the Lucky Queen Poker Hall on Third Street. Leaning against a pole supporting the building's front awning, the pair didn't attract a single bit of attention from the throngs of people that streamed past them.

In fact, those two blended in so perfectly with their surroundings that hardly any of the passersby would even remember seeing them at all. It was their business to stay on the fringe of people's sight that way. Just as it was their business to remain tucked away in the back of other folks' minds like some almost-forgotten dream.

John Grayfeather stood with one shoulder against a post as if it was him instead of the thick timber holding the Lucky Queen up. His muscular six-foot-two-inch frame would have attracted plenty of attention if he'd been doing anything else besides keeping to himself and watching the rest of the town from a distance. Thick, coal-black hair framed a narrow face, then hung all the way down to the middle of his back. Entwined in the shadowy strands were straps of leather tied to bits of eagle bones that rattled together on the rare occasion that the big, full-blooded Sioux moved at all.

The man next to Grayfeather stood just as quietly, making it impossible for any casual observer to tell whether or not he was any acquaintance of the Sioux. Douglas Rhyne had an average build and a forgettable face. His only distinctive feature was a jagged scar spanning the back of his neck. And even that was covered up by his scraggly, shoulder-length brown hair.

Both of them passed the time by puffing on cigarettes, watching the passing crowd move around them with cold, intense eyes. They scanned each and every face like birds of prey waiting to spot that single slow rodent before swooping in for the kill.

But none of the locals seemed to be aware of that fact. Just like those rodents, the other folks walking down the street were too wrapped up in their own lives to worry about what was circling over their heads. And that was just the way Grayfeather and Rhyne liked it.

The sun was a distant memory by the time either of the two men broke the silence between them. It was the Sioux who spoke first. His voice sounded like a storm brewing several miles in the distance.

"You think she'll show?" he asked.

Rhyne took one last drag from his cigarette before flicking it to the street. "Where else is she gonna go? She rode all day to get here and thinks she's safe and sound after tucking herself away. There ain't no place she'd rather be right now . . . unless she knows that we followed her here."

Shaking his head, Grayfeather grunted, "No chance. She ran too fast to get a look over her shoulder. Besides, after what she's done, she thinks she can run faster than death itself."

Laughing in a way that sounded more like an animal choking on a piece of meat, Rhyne hooked his thumbs into his gunbelt and stretched his back. "If she could run that fast, this job might be worth the money we're being paid. As it is, I'm starting to feel bad about charging for such a cakewalk."

"She's not dead yet."

"Yeah, well, we can take care of that quick enough. When do you want to move in?"

· Grayfeather lifted his face to the passing breeze, sampling the air with a well-trained nose. "Not now. It doesn't feel right. I'll let you know when it does."

Pacing in front of the poker hall as a group of local merchants shoved past him, Rhyne fixed his eyes on the Indian. "Well, I've been waiting for your damn signal all night. I say we get this job out of the way so we can collect our money before we spend another night sitting outside like a couple of dogs waiting for scraps."

One moment, Grayfeather was looking at the sky, examining the scarred face of the moon. In the next, he was wheeling around to face Rhyne with a look in his eyes that struck the other man like a fist in his stomach.

"You want to die?" the Sioux asked. "Then go ahead and charge on up there before I say. Believe me, finding another man like you won't be difficult around here. That woman isn't just some helpless little girl."

Rhyne looked nervously around, noticing that they were starting to attract attention from some of the people close to the door. "Fine. Just do whatever you—"

Grayfeather's hands closed around the lapels of Rhyne's coat, pulling him away from prying eyes as if the man inside the clothing was nothing more than a scarecrow. The Sioux pulled him around the building and into a narrow alley. "You're here to do as I say," he rasped. "My people are paying you money to do a job. And I'm here to make sure it gets done right."

"I know that much already," Rhyne said as he reached up to pull the Sioux's hands off him. Even using all his strength, he couldn't come close to breaking free from Grayfeather's hold. "All I'm sayin' is that we could be done with your job a lot quicker if we just bury that woman now since we already know where she is."

The Sioux's grip might have been cast in iron. And as he held Rhyne in his spot, not even the faintest sign of strain appeared on Grayfeather's face. "I don't expect you to know exactly what you're dealing with, white man. But that's not why we're paying you."

Ignoring the pair of stony fists clenched so close to his windpipe, Rhyne managed to pull a confident grin onto his face. "I know exactly what I'm dealing with," he said. "A bunch's Injuns that want to kill some helpless woman."

For a moment, the man's comment went unanswered. Then, Grayfeather's hands unclenched and he allowed the other man to take a step back. Instead of being offended by what he'd heard, the big Sioux merely shook his head and turned to look back at the building across the street.

"Sure," Grayfeather said under his breath. "She's just a helpless woman. Keep telling yourself that as long as it makes you feel better."

FOUR

After he'd spent a few hours inside the familiar walls of Rick's Place, Clint felt his mood take a turn for the better. Of course, the free beers provided by Hartman didn't seem to hurt things any, since the bartender made sure to keep both of the men's mugs full.

Sitting at a table in the back of the room, they whiled away the hours playing a friendly game of cards. Once the nightly crowd started filtering into the saloon, however, that friendly game soon turned into poker. And once that had happened, the stakes began to become progressively greater, until Clint didn't have time to think about what had been rattling around inside his mind earlier that afternoon.

After he'd completely lost himself in the fine art of betting and bluffing, Clint felt as though everything was right in the world. And it only got better once the showgirls started working their way through the crowd, sitting on familiar laps when they weren't kicking their skirts up on stage.

"So what do you say, Clint?" Hartman asked after he was dealt his most recent hand.

Fanning his own cards in front of him, Clint shrugged and said, "I think I'm in for a dollar."

"Not that. I mean about what we were talking about earlier."

"Oh, that. As much as I hate to admit it, I think you're actually right about something for a change. It's too damn hard to sit around thinking about things like that when I'd much rather just sit back and let them happen."

Suddenly, there was a clinking sound of another pile of chips joining the others in the middle of the table. "Sorry to break this up," said one of the others in the game. "But are we here to play cards or shoot the breeze?"

Clint threw in his money with an apologetic shrug. "Sorry about that. Just squaring some old business away."

"Aww," Hartman groaned as he twisted his face up in a pained scowl. "There's that word again. Business. Ain't it bad enough that my back aches every other time I lift a keg out of the cellar, or do you have to keep rubbing salt in my wounds to boot?"

The entire table got a laugh out of that, and the betting continued. Clint played through the next couple of hands feeling something he hadn't felt for a good long time. Finally, he allowed himself to take his eyes away from every soul that walked through the front door. Finally, his right arm didn't twitch toward his gun at every loud noise. And after a while, he was even able to forget about the weight of the modified Colt hanging at his side.

The stack of cards was set down in front of Clint after having been cut by the man beside him. Clint reached out and felt the weight of them in his hands, and was just about to start dealing when he spotted a pair of shadowy figures standing just outside the saloon's front door.

Neither of the figures was doing anything besides taking up space, but there was something about them that didn't set right in Clint's head. Something about their perfect stillness that seemed somehow . . . unnatural. Almost

as if they were a couple of blocky statues guarding the
door where nobody but him knew they were there.

A pair of statues with their features all but lost in the
dim light, leaving nothing to be seen but eyes, which
flicked back and forth over every other person in the saloon. Even from where he was, Clint could see the men
were armed, but so were nearly all the others within the
crowded building.

Just as one of the figures looked in his direction, Clint
heard a familiar voice that broke his concentration.

"Hey, Clint," Hartman said. "You going to deal or just
hold them cards for yourself?"

Clint shook his head a bit and started tossing cards to
each of the men seated around the table. He didn't say a
word through the entire hand, responding only with a nod
as the other players bet their money and asked for cards
to replace the ones they'd discarded. Even though he was
distracted, Clint managed to win the hand with a straight
flush.

After the cards were passed to one of the other players
at the table, Hartman leaned in closer to Clint and asked,
"Are you all right?"

"Yeah. Sure."

"Then rake in your chips before one of these others
decides to do it for you."

Clint reached out and pulled his winnings in front of
him just in time for the next antes to be thrown into the
middle of the table. He could feel Hartman's eyes on him,
and knew what question would be coming next without
his friend even having to ask it. "Those two by the door,"
Clint said while motioning with a nod toward the right
direction. "Do you know them?"

Hartman craned his neck to get a look. "Nope," he said
after a few seconds. "Can't say as I do. But that doesn't
mean they haven't been in here before."

"Well, they've been looking over this room like a couple of vultures for the last hour or so. At least, that's when I first noticed them."

"You think they might be trouble?"

Thinking back over the last couple of days, Clint thought for a second that he might just be making too much out of something as a way to justify his hankering to move out of Labyrinth. But when he took another look at the shadowy pair, Clint knew that there was something else that was giving him the uneasy feeling in the back of his head. "They're looking for someone," he said. "And I don't think they're just meeting them for drinks."

"All right," Hartman said while leaning back in his chair and taking a glance at his cards. "You want me to ask them to leave?"

"No," Clint replied as he turned his attention back to the game. "If they're content to stay put, then I'm content to keep an eye on them from here. It could be nothing."

"You think so?"

Clint fanned his cards and tossed a minimum bet into the pot. "No. I don't."

FIVE

Darryl Besskin stepped inside the small hotel room, shut the door, and slid the latch into place. Turning slowly around, he reached out and twisted the knob on the lantern until a dim, warm glow pushed the shadows back a little farther into the dusty corners. The light was only a slight improvement over total darkness, but it was still enough to touch each of the four walls of the cramped space.

The hotel was the cheapest in town, and only half a glance would tell someone why. The walls were thin. The rooms were barely larger than closets, and some of the beds were actually less comfortable than sleeping on a rock.

But Darryl wasn't about to sleep on the bed he'd rented. In fact, with the way his blood was pumping through his veins and his heart slammed inside his chest, he doubted he'd be getting much sleep at all for a good part of the night.

The dim orange glow of the lantern pushed through the room until it played over the smooth, delicate contours of a woman who lay on her side on a pile of pillows stacked up on the middle of the bed. Her body was slender and tightly packed; breasts small yet firm, stomach muscled and trim.

When the light fell over her, the young woman rolled onto her stomach, squirming slightly as though the flickering illumination was another man's hand caressing the edge of her hips. Instead of covering herself up, she succeeded in making herself appear even more alluring as every contour of her body was framed by the warm glow. The firm, rounded curve of her buttocks was highlighted by equal parts of light and shadow.

"What took you so long?" she asked in a quiet voice.

Darryl was already unbuckling his gunbelt and tossing it to the floor as he made his way toward the bed. "I had to settle some business first," he said, his eyes not even attempting to meet hers. "Now that all that's over, I can have you all to myself."

The girl smiled and wrapped her arms around a pillow, clutching it to her breasts and closing her eyes. Arching her back made her round bottom seem even more perfect. And judging by the smile on her face, she might have been in a luxury suite rather than a West Texas dive.

"Could you turn the light out?" she asked. "I get bashful sometimes."

Darryl smiled and unbuttoned his shirt. "You got nothing to be bashful about, girl. I want to get a good, long look at ya."

First, she propped herself up onto her elbows, and then onto her knees. Straightening her back, she dropped the pillow and let his eyes wander over her body before she crossed her arms across her breasts. Although the look in Emma's eyes carried a bit of shyness, there was something much more seductive in the way she turned her face down just a bit and ran the tip of her tongue fleetingly over her bottom lip.

Emma's skin had a moonlit glow about it, which was made even more striking by the sleek darkness of the soft hair flowing down past her shoulder blades. Her hips twitched invitingly as she moved over the mattress and pressed herself up against Darryl's body.

"I'd rather be in the dark," she whispered. "It makes me more comfortable that way."

Darryl instinctively moved toward the lantern, but was just able to stop himself before he reached out and twisted the knob. "Then you're just going to have to do it yourself," he said finally.

Nodding subtly, Emma got down on her hands and knees, letting her hair drape down to cover her breasts, and crawled backward off the bed. When she stood, her small pink nipples stood erect just beneath the strands of her hair. This time, when she tried to cover herself, her hands gently brushed over her skin, lingering in the spots where she liked to be touched. After making her way to the lantern, she turned and ran her fingertips over the patch of hair between her legs, taking a quick intake of breath when her fingernail brushed over the lips of her pussy.

"You're beautiful," Darryl managed to say as he watched the girl pleasure herself across the room.

Emma had lost herself for a few seconds within the sensations that rushed through her body as her fingers made tiny circles around her sensitive clit. As her skin became slick with anticipation, she bit her lower lip and reached out to turn the light off.

"There," she said softly. "That's a lot better."

Although he couldn't see much more than the outline of her body in what little light came through the grimy window, Darryl heard every step she took as she came back to him. Finally, he felt her hands slip inside his shirt and wrap around his midsection. The delicate press of her lips against his chest brought a satisfied groan from the back of his throat.

Darryl held his arms out to allow her to remove his

shirt, and then immediately took her inside his embrace.
Emma's body felt fragile and warm against his skin. He
let his hands roam over her back and down the curve of
her spine until he could cup the firm roundness of her
bottom.

Kissing him along his neck and down over his muscular
chest, Emma savored the feel of Darryl's hands on her
body and allowed herself to give in to the desires surging
through her flesh. Her hands worked quickly to pull his
pants down over his hips, and she lowered herself onto
her knees to finish the task.

Once she was down there, she could feel the heat em-
anating from his body, her hands drifting instinctively to
his stiff cock. She stroked him with firm, even motions,
and felt him grow even harder as she leaned in closer to
run the tip of her tongue along his shaft.

When Emma closed her lips around the tip of his penis,
she felt Darryl's hands come down on her shoulders as
though that was the only thing keeping him up. She
looked up at him then, finding nothing but a shape looming in the darkness. Even so, she could tell he was looking
back down at her as one of his hands moved from her
shoulder to stroke her hair.

Closing her eyes and focusing on the responses she got
from her lover, Emma took all of his cock into her mouth,
bobbing her head back and forth while circling him with
her tongue. All the while, her hands wrapped around behind him, pulling him in closer until she swallowed him
whole.

Darryl's knees started to buckle as the intensity of his
pleasure grew stronger and stronger. Although he almost
hated to do it, he reached down and gently moved Emma
back. Taking her by the hands, he guided her to her feet
and toward the bed.

"I don't want this to be over yet, darlin'," he said.

Once she was lying down in front of him, Emma saw

the looming figure descend upon her until she could make
out the expression on his face silhouetted by the pale
moonlight. Acting purely on impulse, she spread her legs
and allowed him to settle between them. The thick muscle
between his legs pressed against her damp vagina.

Darryl held still for a moment, savoring the feel of her
body against his own. One of his hands reached out to
close around her slender wrist while the other took its time
feeling along the side of her body. Emma's small breast
fit perfectly in his hand, and she let out a disappointed
sigh when he moved it away.

Feeling the muscles in her stomach tense beneath his
touch, Darryl leaned in close to Emma's ear. "What's the
matter?" he asked. "You feel like you're about to burst."

"I am," she groaned. "I can't wait another second."

SIX

Normally, when Clint was sitting at a poker game, he was aware of every little thing going on in the faces of the other players. He was a master in the art of looking for signs that would let him know if one of the others was bluffing or ready to unleash a royal flush. Being aware of signs was what separated a good cardplayer from an easy mark for the sharks.

Tonight, however, Clint didn't even know the names of the other two men at the table with himself and Rick Hartman. Luckily, he wasn't expecting to cash out with enough for a retirement fund either.

Hartman tossed enough to cover his bet onto the pile of chips in the middle of the table, and turned to look at his friend. "They still there?" he asked.

Nodding, Clint glared across the saloon at the pair that were still haunting the front door like a couple of gargoyles. "Yep. But it's getting crowded in here, so I can't tell what they're watching."

"Then why don't you just go out there and introduce yourself?"

The betting went around the table a few more times, and Clint was raking in another stack of winnings before he responded. "I'm pretty sure they're not after anyone in here, and there's no sense in giving them a reason to move until they see what they are after. That way I can follow them and see what's got their attention."

"And you also save me from having to clean up after another gunfight," Hartman said while nodding appreciatively. "Thanks a lot."

"Hopefully it won't get to that, but yes . . . I wouldn't want to do any more damage to this place."

As he thought back to the last time someone had come after Clint in his saloon, Hartman shuddered and clenched his teeth at the same time. "On second thought . . . if you've got such a bad feeling about them fellas, why don't you get them the hell away from here right now?"

"If you insist," Clint replied as he pushed away from the table and got to his feet. "But I must say you're getting a bit skittish in your old age." Before Hartman could respond, Clint slapped his friend on the back and headed toward the door. "Watch those chips for me," he said over his shoulder. "I'll be right back."

Grayfeather stood in the darkness, letting the crowd pass to and fro around him, not taking his eyes from the shoddy structure across the street. His arms were folded imperiously across his chest and his back was ramrod straight, giving him the bearing of a regal sculpture.

On the other side of the doorway, Rhyne shifted on his feet and looked from the Sioux to the activity going on inside the building behind him. "Are we going in or what?" he asked for the thousandth time.

Grayfeather said nothing in response, just as he had the many other times he'd been asked that question.

Like an impatient child, Rhyne stared at the other man and slammed his fist against the wall behind him. "Then I'm leaving. Wave to me or something when you want to do something besides stand out in the dark and watch. I didn't get paid to waste my time like—"

"Enough," Grayfeather said.

That single word struck Rhyne like a swat on the nose, stopping him in mid-tirade.

The Sioux stared at the same spot he'd been watching the entire time. After a few more seconds had passed, he lifted a finger and pointed it toward the rickety building. "It's time."

Even though Rhyne had been itching to move, he couldn't help but look nervously between the opposite building and the towering Indian. "How do you know?"

"That's why I came with you," Grayfeather replied simply. "Because I know. We'd better get going. There's not a lot of time."

Rhyne let out an aggravated sigh. "We would've had plenty of time if you'd have just—"

But it was no use. The Sioux was already walking across the street in swift, massive strides. When Grayfeather left his spot, a few of the people nearby jumped, as though they already written off the Indian as something carved from a log. One of them started to say something, but quickly bit his tongue when he saw Grayfeather reach beneath the tunic he wore to produce a short, yet deadly-looking tomahawk.

Following in the Sioux's steps, Rhyne kept his own weapon hidden until they reached the cover of the run-down building's interior. Once he was away from prying eyes, he snatched a .44-caliber revolver from the holster at his waist.

"All right," Rhyne said as he hurried to get in front of Grayfeather. "I'll take the lead. Just try not to get in my way."

The Sioux lifted the tomahawk and set it on his shoulder. Gesturing with his other hand, he said, "Of course. After you."

Rhyne didn't take his eyes from the Sioux until that tomahawk came back down. Heading for a set of stairs in one corner of the front room, he shook his head and muttered, "Damn Injuns," under his breath.

Clint had been taking his time walking across the saloon. Not wanting to draw any attention to himself until it was absolutely necessary, he made a beeline for the door without once taking his eyes from the figures standing there.

He was just over halfway there when he turned his head for a second to make sure he didn't knock some staggering drunk off his feet. When he casually looked back again, one of the figures was gone and the other was just taking off at a quick trot.

Clint swore in a barely audible snarl and abandoned his hope of making it to the door without being noticed. Instead, he started pushing people out of his way until he bolted outside into the cool night air. It took a moment for his eyes to adjust to the darkness, but as soon as he could focus, he saw two familiar figures stepping onto the boardwalk across the street.

Even with just the moon and a few sputtering lanterns on the side of the street to guide him, Clint could plainly see that both men were armed. Not only that, but they were drawing their weapons as they slowly approached the building across from Rick's Place.

"So much for the quiet approach," Clint said to himself as he charged into the street and got ready to draw.

SEVEN

Emma's body felt so soft and fragile beneath Darryl's that for a moment he was afraid he might break her. But as he pushed his hips between her legs and slid his cock inside her, he could feel every muscle in the girl's body tense and her fingernails dig into the backs of his shoulders.

"Oh, God," she moaned as her legs wrapped tightly around him. "Feels so good."

Darryl pushed forward until he'd buried himself all the way inside her. At that point, Emma's legs tightened even more as she thrust her hips forward, grinding against his thick shaft. The sounds of her ragged breath filled the dark room, and once Darryl started pumping in a steady rhythm, that sound was joined by the flimsy headboard pounding against the wall.

Every time he pumped inside her, Darryl could feel Emma getting wetter and wetter as her cries became louder and louder. Before he reached his climax, Darryl pulled out of her and said, "Roll over."

She pouted slightly and reached down to try and coax him back inside, but she couldn't get him to do what she wanted. Even though she knew she could get him to do

whatever she desired with a few of the right words, Emma
also knew what Darryl had in mind for her.

As she gathered her legs beneath her, she let her toes
slide over the skin of his thighs. Emma then took her time
twisting onto her stomach, and once she was there, she
pressed her face against a pillow and propped her behind
up in the air.

Darryl looked down at her, drinking in the sight of her
body outlined in the pale light of the moon. Lines of
shadow flowed over her bare skin, making the round
curve of her backside look all the more inviting. Unable
to simply look at her any longer, he grabbed hold of her
hips with both hands and pulled her closer to him so he
could slide his cock between her legs.

Clenching the pillow in tight little fists, Emma moaned
softly when she felt Darryl's thick penis move over her
flesh and bury itself deep into her vagina. His strong
hands held her tightly as she pushed herself back against
him and forced him as deep inside as he could go.

When he began pounding into her, Emma reached
around and clasped her hands behind her back. It didn't
take more than a few seconds for Darryl to pick up on
the hint and grab hold of her wrists in one hand. The
feeling of being restrained brought a louder groan from
the depths of Emma's body, and within minutes she could
feel the first tingles of orgasm creeping in around the
edges of her body.

As her blood started rushing quicker beneath her flesh,
all she could hear was the flood of her breath pumping
through her lungs and the deafening sound of her own
passionate cries.

She couldn't hear Darryl calling out her name as he
thrust desperately between her legs.

She couldn't hear the bed scraping against the loose
floorboards.

She couldn't even hear the crash of the door to their room being kicked in by a single, well-placed boot.

Clint thought for a moment that he could hear something strange coming from the building across the street. Although the gambling and saloon district was always noisy at this time of night, there was something beneath it all that caught his attention more than anything else.

If he'd had more time to think about it, Clint might have tried to figure out what that sound was. But since he seemed to have more than enough to occupy himself for the moment, he put the noise aside and focused in on the task at hand.

"You there," he called out to the men who'd been skulking near the entrance to Rick's Place for the better part of the night. "Is there something I can help you with?"

Clint hadn't put a lot of thought into the question. In fact, all he'd wanted to do was break the silence that had formed between himself and the pair that had darted across the street. He didn't even expect a response.

But a response was what he got.

Before Clint could even tell that either of the other men had stopped moving, one of them swiveled around in a cyclone of black duster and long hair, both hands rising up from his sides, each one clenched around a revolver. Both guns erupted in a spout of fire and smoke, the thundering shots echoing in every direction.

Clint's instincts had been on edge all night long, and as he dove to the ground without even having to think about what he was doing, he thanked those instincts for saving his hide yet again. Hot lead whipped through the air over his head as Clint dropped and rolled to the left toward a nearby water trough.

When he got his feet beneath him again, Clint's hand was filled with his modified Colt. He didn't remember drawing it, but knew it would be in his grasp when he needed it. Although the trough wasn't high enough to cover him unless he was lying flat on his back, Clint used the dark to his advantage to throw the gunman off his aim.

Before firing a single round, Clint took a moment to strain his ears for any trace of where the gunmen were headed. The one who'd shot at him was clomping noisily on the boardwalk in an attempt to get Clint back in his sights. But as for the other one . . .

Rather than waste another moment on guesswork, Clint turned on his heels so he could see his targets. Unfortunately, the noise his boots made against the loose gravel combined with the motion of his body was more than enough to give away his location.

More shots blazed through the air. While most of them went wild, some managed to punch holes into Clint's trough, and a select few got close enough to him that he threw himself face-down into the dirt until it was safe to move again.

As he pressed his cheek against the cold ground and the thunder roared inches above him, Clint swore to never again doubt the predictive powers of paranoia.

EIGHT

Emma screamed as her entire world became a chaotic jumble of sparking gunshot flashes and the deafening sounds of war. Guns exploded only a few feet away from her ears. Voices raised in cries of pain and blood lust. The floor and ceiling spun around her as she felt herself tumbling off the bed and onto the chipped wooden planks below.

"Emma, get out of here!" someone screamed at her.

For a moment, Emma wasn't even sure who'd called out her name. There was a stark moment of terror at the thought that the invaders knew her so well, but then she recognized Darryl's voice amid all the terrifying confusion.

She wanted to respond, but Emma couldn't get her body to obey her commands. Her brain pleaded for her to flee, fight back, find Darryl, do anything, but her muscles were frozen in place.

The gunshots kept blasting around her, and the only thing she could do was crawl under the bed and cover her ears.

• • •

Smoke from his .44 drifted up from the burning muzzle
and stung at the corners of his eyes. The smell of it was
more familiar to him than the scent of fresh air, and it
brought with it more memories than anything else in the
world. His hand was steady as a rock wrapped around
that pistol, and he reloaded it with a quick gesture of his
hands and a few flicks of his wrists.

Behind him, Grayfeather filled up the doorway enough
to block out most of the light filtering in from the hall.
"Is she dead?" he asked.

Rhyne stepped over to the bed and reached down for
the body that was still twitching in its final death throes
upon the soiled sheets. Reaching down to pull up the person by the hair, Rhyne knew instantly that the body was
too heavy to be the one he was after. Just to be on the
safe side, however, he pushed the barrel of the .44 against
the person's skull and emptied it with a single pull of his
trigger.

Not wanting to take his eyes away from the hunt, the
killer let the body drop and gestured over his shoulder
toward the Sioux. "Turn that lantern up," Rhyne said as
he stalked around the bed.

Grayfeather's steps thumped against the floor as he
stepped closer to the room's single lantern. Although the
hall wasn't lit much better, the difference was enough to
make him stop for a second and let his eyes adjust to the
near-total darkness. After no more than a few seconds
went by, Grayfeather was able to make out distinct shapes
in the shadows. One of them was the lantern, and he
reached for it and twisted the knob once he found it.

The first thing to catch the Sioux's attention was the
body lying on the bed. It wasn't the first corpse he'd ever
seen, but it was easily one of the messiest. Once Grayfeather was certain the body wasn't a woman's, he turned
to look at Rhyne, who was pacing around to the other
side of the bed.

"This is her room," the Sioux said. "I know she was in here."

Rhyne's voice snapped out impatiently. "I know it too, goddammit! But that doesn't help me much." The gunman's pulse was just starting to quiet down enough for him to focus in on what he was doing. Also, the flashes left from the gunshots were just starting to fade from his eyes.

Rhyne was just noticing that the room was barely big enough to hold both himself and Grayfeather. In fact, he nearly backed out of the open window as he tried to examine what he thought was another couple feet of floor space.

"Turn the light up, for Christ's sake," Rhyne growled. "As soon as I can see, I'll be able to put that bitch down for good."

That last sentence felt like an icy claw tightening around Emma's stomach. She was starting to feel as though she was going to pass out, which could have been from the fear coursing through her soul, or the fact that she refused to take more than half a breath in order to keep as quiet as possible.

She pressed herself tightly against the dusty floor beneath the bed, willing her thin body to lie flat against the wooden planks. Even though dust swirled up into her nose and the occasional spider scurried across the backs of her legs, she managed to keep from making a sound.

She knew that any sound would bring the killers to her that much quicker. At least in the darkness, she felt she might be able to hide from them. But now, as light from the lantern grew in the room around her, Emma knew that she had nowhere to go.

There was nothing for her to do besides wait for one of the men to look beneath the bed in the cramped room's only real hiding place.

Even as these thoughts raced through her mind, there was still a part of her that schemed for a way to escape what had happened to Darryl. That part forced her eyes open to search for any possible chance that might prolong her life . . . if even for a few more seconds.

Still naked and covered in dust, she had no means to fight them.

She couldn't think clearly enough to try and talk her way out.

So that left only one option.

The killers' footsteps rattled the floor beneath Emma's stomach, causing more dust to puff up from between the boards and into her face. Tears stung the corners of her eyes, nearly causing her to make a sound. She fought back the impulse to sniffle or even whimper, swearing that the men in her room could hear her hair brush against the ground when she turned her head to look at the front door.

Snippets of the killers' conversation drifted into her ears, which only lent more strength to the muscles tensed beneath her skin.

". . . bitch is dead . . ."

". . . might have jumped out the window . . ."

". . . check the bed before you leave . . ."

If she needed anything else to convince her to act, those last words were it. In the back of her mind, Emma counted down the last remaining moments of her life while she took one more frantic look at the bottom of the room.

Three.

One set of boots thumped around behind her. Another set still stood by the table where the lantern was. The front door had swung halfway open to reveal a glimpse of the hallway, which beckoned to her like a view of the promised land.

Two.

Emma never thought the second man would leave the door unguarded for so long, even though it had only been less than a minute since the lantern had been turned up. Not wanting to waste another moment, Emma coiled her legs as best she could behind her . . .

One.

. . . and pushed herself out from beneath the bed.

Slivers of wood dug into her bare flesh as she slid over the floor. Rough edges of loose boards tore jagged pieces from her skin, and one of her fingernails was even torn out as she clawed her way from beneath the bloody mattress, but she ignored all of that as she moved toward the waiting door.

The killers were yelling something, but Emma didn't hear anything but the howl of crazed animals biting at her heels. When she sensed open space over her head once again, she tried to lift herself onto her feet so she could move that much faster.

A gunshot blasted through the air, followed by another. Either bullet would have dug into her back if not for the fact that Emma's uncertain footing caused her to stumble awkwardly, forcing her almost back down to the ground. Catching herself with the palms of her hands and pushing forward with her feet, Emma made it out of the room and into the hall.

She almost stopped for a second to try and decide which way to turn, but the survival instincts inside her mind were like spurs in her sides, forcing her onward as fast as she could possibly go.

NINE

Rhyne was halfway bent over and already starting to pull the bed up off the floor when he saw the burst of frenzied motion on the floor. Since he'd been expecting to find the woman under there anyway, he was quick to drop the bed and take a shot at her before she could get away.

Aiming for a head shot, he squeezed the trigger just as she all but fell flat on her face. His bullet punched into the door across the hall, but he was already taking another shot. That one was hurried and she was still moving too wildly to be targeted properly, so it also dug into a nearby wall.

"Shit!" he hollered.

Grayfeather watched her with mild amusement, taking his time to cock the tomahawk back near his right ear. Waiting until she paused for a second in the hall, he fixed his eyes on the spot between her shoulder blades and snapped his elbow like he was cracking a whip.

The tomahawk whistled through the air with lethal perfection.

His target, which had been heading in one direction, suddenly decided to go the other. It was almost as though

37

she knew what was coming her way and had called on her reserves to avoid it.

Landing with a solid *thunk,* the tomahawk's blade dug into the wall, causing the feathers tied around its handle to dance against the handle's smooth surface.

"I swear I'm gonna kill that bitch!" Rhyne screamed as he started climbing over the bed.

Grayfeather held out one massive arm and plucked the gunman from the air. "No," he said. "Let her go."

"What?"

"You heard me," the Sioux replied while pushing Rhyne back against the windowsill. "Her medicine is too strong right now. If it was possible to kill her this night, one of us would have done it."

"She got lucky is all. I could chase her down and put a bullet through her skull right now if—"

Grayfeather turned and locked Rhyne in place with a murderous stare. "You'll . . . do . . . as . . . I . . . say." Once he was certain the defiance had been snuffed out of the gunman's eyes, Grayfeather allowed his normal calm to return. Looking to the body on top of the bed, he said, "She's already caused one man's death. We'll just have to wait for a time when her poison isn't flowing as strong."

As she ran down the hall, Emma didn't think about the fact that she was naked and pumping her arms like a madwoman. She didn't think about the rough floor chewing up the bottoms of her feet. She didn't even think about how close the killers could be behind her.

All she worried about was running.

By the time she realized she'd even made it to the staircase at the end of the hall, she was already halfway down it. Emma stumbled and nearly fell down the last five steps, but she somehow managed to catch herself and run some more.

Finally, she caught sight of the front door out of the blurred corners of her vision. Ignoring the wide eyes staring at her from the few people venturing out of their rooms after hearing the gunshots, Emma threw open the door and bolted outside.

When some of the fresh outside air was pulled into her lungs, she looked for the closest hiding place she could find, ran toward it, and then changed her direction once she was under cover of shadows. She hoped the killers would waste their time looking for her in the alley she'd ducked into as she ran all the way down that alley to emerge on the other side.

Now was the time to look for her real hiding spot.

Her mind raced for someplace that would be the last place the killers would look. At that moment, she heard the crackle of more gunshots in the distance. The noise wasn't coming from her hotel, and she had no idea what might have brought about even more shooting on this of all nights. All she did know was that she didn't want to be around any more guns.

Then she realized that the killers would assume she'd be thinking that same thing.

As much as she hated to do it, Emma gathered up her courage and started moving through the darkness toward the shots being fired no more than a few blocks away. Strangely enough, while she headed in that direction, Emma felt an odd calm fall down over her shoulders. It was as though her guardian angel was patting her on the back, assuring her that she was making the right decision.

She moved from alley to alley, doing her best to ignore the familiar voices coming from the shoddy hotel where she'd been screaming with passion less than an hour before. At the back of one building, someone had hung out their clothes to dry after cleaning them. Emma helped herself to a simple cotton dress, and sent out another quiet prayer thanking whatever angel had seen her through this far.

Emma wasn't much of a spiritual woman, but at times like these it was hard to deny the fact that there was something else going on that couldn't quite be seen or touched. Its effects could be seen, but the source always remained just out of reach.

Folks had been telling her for as long as she could remember that that force was something evil. At times, even she might have been inclined to agree with them. Those folks would have been the first ones to tell her that what had happened tonight . . . what had happened to Darryl . . . could have been nothing but her own fault.

There were those who'd told her she was cursed.

But how could she be cursed and also be delivered from death's grasp the way she had been tonight?

Emma thought about those things as a way to keep herself from getting too scared about the danger she was in at that moment. It was a way to keep her mind away from the killers on her trail and on the road ahead.

Since there wasn't a whole lot else for her to do, she wrapped her arms around herself and kept heading for the sound of gunfire.

TEN

Waiting for the shots to stop coming, Clint gathered his legs up beneath him until he was squatting down behind the water trough. After a few more seconds rolled by, the men shooting at him had to stop and reload, giving Clint just enough time to throw himself into a forward roll away from his flimsy cover.

When he came to a stop, his feet were planted on the ground and he was able to straighten up to a normal stance. Twisting on the balls of his feet, Clint turned until he caught sight of the closest shooter. He pointed the Colt at the man as though he was simply pointing his finger at the target, let out a breath, and squeezed the trigger.

The pistol bucked once in his hand, barking in the sound that Clint knew almost as well as his own voice. Not waiting long enough to watch the first man drop, Clint was in motion once again and running across the street to the building where the second man had gone.

He knew he hadn't killed the first man, but Clint was still surprised that that one was standing by the time he made it to his side. Just to be sure, Clint cocked his arm back and sent the bottom of his fist sailing toward that shooter's head. He connected with the Colt's handle di-

41

rectly onto the other man's temple, causing the figure to collapse like a bag of rocks onto the street.

Hearing the impact the first man made when he fell, Clint moved on to the boardwalk, where he could see the second man's back retreating into the building directly in front of him. Clint didn't have to look at any signs to know that the building was a cheap boardinghouse that was also a frequent haunt of the working girls who didn't like to conduct business in a room over a saloon.

At the first sound of gunfire, most of the patrons had found good places to hide. But there were still a few who poked their heads out with curiosity as the noisy exchange wore on. One of those faces turned toward Clint as he rushed through the front door, regarding him with a mixture of fear and awe.

"Where'd he go?" Clint asked the frightened face.

"That way, Mr. Adams," came the squeaky reply, followed by a finger pointing toward one of the nearby rooms. "He ran in there."

Clint recognized the face as belonging to one of Labyrinth's aldermen who acted as a go-between with local businesses and the mayor. More than likely, the woman crouched behind the chair next to him was a "gift" from a store owner who was hoping to get some kind of deal from the influential mediator.

"Thanks a lot, Bill," Clint said with a tip of his hat.

The alderman looked like a kid who just realized he still had his hand in the cookie jar, and turned a guilty eye toward the prostitute at his side.

Storing away the chance meeting for later, Clint rushed to the door the alderman had indicated, which was still swinging back and forth on old hinges. Clint knew better than to charge right in after a desperate man, so he ducked to one side at the last second to press his back against the wall beside the door's frame.

The instant before his shoulders hit the wall, two shots

came in quick procession to punch fresh holes through the flimsy wood. Gritting his teeth and edging away from the door a step or two, Clint brought the Colt up and listened for any hint of what the other man was doing inside the room.

For a moment, he could only hear the leftover sounds of gunfire. But then his ears picked out the traces of wood scraping against wood. Glass rattled slightly in a frame.

The man was opening a window, Clint decided. More than likely, the shooter already had one foot out and was about to drop onto the ground outside the boardinghouse.

Clint wasn't about to let the man get away that easily. Not after he'd been forced to abandon a perfectly good poker game to chase him.

After giving the man in the other room just enough time to get in a position that would be hard to get out of right away, Clint pushed the door open and waved his hand in the open space to see if he could provoke another round of nervous gunfire.

All he got in response was a few strange looks from the alderman, who was still watching from his spot closer to the front door. Clint crouched down low and stepped into the doorway with his Colt ready to respond at a moment's notice.

He saw right away that the pistol wouldn't be needed, especially since the figure was straddling the windowsill. The other man's legs were hanging on opposite sides of the outside wall, his hands grabbing hold of whatever they could to keep him from spilling off his tenuous perch.

"Going somewhere?" Clint asked as he tapped the barrel of the gun against the wall near the other man's head.

Hearing that, the figure let out a surprised yelp and let go of the wall so he could scramble for the gun at his side.

Clint slapped the Colt back into its holster just as fast as he'd drawn it, and was able to catch the man by the scruff of the neck before he toppled out into the street. For a second, Clint thought the other man's weight might just be enough to pull him out of the window as well. But he was able to plant his feet at just the right time, enabling him to drag the second man back inside.

Turning his upper body as he pulled, Clint pulled the man off the windowsill and pitched him onto the bed. It was only at that time that he saw the young man and woman huddled in the corner near a pile of rumpled clothes.

"Sorry about this," Clint said after the other man landed heavily upon the bed. "But you might want to find another room. Maybe the alderman's is free."

Realizing that they weren't going to be hurt after all, the couple skittered across the floor and ran for the nearby set of stairs.

"As for you," Clint said to the man at the other end of his clenched fist, "I'd suggest you come up with a damn good explanation for all of this and be ready to talk after we go collect your friend."

Before he could say a word, the figure was hauled back to his feet and dragged back outside the boardinghouse, where his partner was just starting to pull himself onto his hands and knees.

ELEVEN

Grayfeather didn't have to look at the man behind him to know that Rhyne was fuming. The Sioux could feel the gunman's anger like waves of heat searing into his back from a fire that had been set an arm's length away. The killer grumbled like a petulant child every so often, mumbling threats and promises leveled at the woman that had managed to slip from out of their combined grasp.

"Don't it get to you?" Rhyne asked once they'd put some distance between themselves and the cheap hotel.

They were searching the surrounding area, looking for any trace of the woman. So far, they'd found a couple of likely spots as well as a few locals who said they'd seen the naked girl flying down the street as though her heels were on fire, but they had yet to find Emma herself. Now they were searching Labyrinth by walking in widening circles with the hotel at their center.

Grayfeather nudged aside a stack of broken lumber at the foot of an alley before he responded to Rhyne. "What are you asking me?"

"I want to know how come you let that bitch go back there."

"I'm the one leading this hunt, so you don't—"

"No," Rhyne snapped. "I do need to ask about it. We had that woman in our sights. Sure, she was lucky enough to get out of the room without catching a bullet, but she wouldn't have made it another twenty yards if you'd have just let me go after her."

"So you say."

Their search had taken them a block away from the hotel by this time. They were in a quiet section of Labyrinth that was mainly stores and a few homes nestled in between the town's livelier districts. Rhyne stepped up to the Sioux with his hand poised over the .44 hanging at his hip.

"Yeah," the gunman snarled. "That's exactly what I say."

Grayfeather looked down on the smaller man as though Rhyne was a bug that he was thinking of squashing.

"You know what I think?" Rhyne continued. "I think you've been watching that pretty thing a little too long and have gone a little sweet on her. Maybe you even like standing outside her window, knowing that she's inside fucking like the little whore she—"

Snapping out like a snake's tongue, Grayfeather's hand took hold of the front of Rhyne's shirt and pulled him off balance with quiet, controlled strength. For the next few moments, Grayfeather simply held Rhyne in place as though he was dangling the other man over a cliff. His eyes locked onto Rhyne's and when the other man started to talk, the Sioux merely had to shake his head to get him to shut his mouth once again.

"You have a wicked tongue for such a simple man," Grayfeather said finally. "I don't appreciate having to hear all of the filth that pours out of it. So before I say anything else, let me tell you that I'll remove that tongue of yours if you don't control it."

The Sioux waited for a few seconds to see if Rhyne would be dumb enough to test him right then and there.

He didn't think the gunman would try his patience, and he was right. All Rhyne did in response to the threat was hang from the Indian's hand and stare back at him through narrow, smoldering eyes.

"Good," Grayfeather said with a curt nod. "Now I'd also appreciate it if you'd never refer to Miss Deerborne that way. Just because we must kill her doesn't mean that we have to commit the act like savages."

Silence fell back upon the two men like a thick blanket. The tension between them faded away, and eventually dwindled down to something much more manageable.

"You gonna let me go now?" Rhyne asked after a while.

Grayfeather responded by opening his fist and allowing the other man to take a couple of steps back. Once Grayfeather was fairly certain that he wouldn't have to defend himself right away, the Sioux crossed his arms over his chest and waited.

"Tell me something, red man," Rhyne said, referring to Grayfeather the way he had at their first meeting. "Either you don't expect to find this woman right now or you don't want to. Which is it?"

If Grayfeather heard the question, he didn't give any indication. Instead, he just looked down his nose. The occasional blink of his eyes was the only sign that he was alive at all and not some statue that had been magically running about for the last couple of days. After a few uncomfortable seconds passed by, the Sioux craned his neck to look toward the sound made by a cat searching through a pile of trash.

"I told you before," the Indian said. "She wields strong medicine. Some of your people call it magic, but more of them call it luck."

Rhyne's face broke into a wide, tainted grin. "Finally we agree on something. That girl has a lucky streak even longer than *your* arm."

"And that is how she survives. When she uses her medicine, it can work for her just as strongly as it works against others."

Gunfire popped in another part of town, followed by the muffled sound of raised voices. The pair were too far away to hear what was being said, but they could tell plenty by the tone of the shouting. Both men turned to look in the direction the shots had come from, regarding them as though the shots were just as normal as crickets chirping on a hot summer night.

"Sounds like the boys we hired are keeping their end up," Rhyne pointed out. "You think they found who they were supposed to find?"

"Clint Adams?" Grayfeather said. "It doesn't matter now."

Shrugging, Rhyne kicked at a stray pebble. "Guess not."

They started walking casually down the alley, and made it all the way to the other end before the Sioux spoke again.

"To answer your question . . . I let her get away because I didn't like the way things were turning out. That's why I'm leading this hunt. I have instincts you could never even know about. And all it takes is one wrong step for us to wind up as dead as the man we found in her room."

Rhyne laughed in such a way that made his shoulders jump up around his ears. "Sorry to be the one to tell you this . . . but I killed that man back there."

"You were the weapon, but what caused you to strike down that man after leaving so many others you could have shot with less effort? That is the woman's medicine. She twists fate to do her bidding, making her just as deadly as the gun in your hand."

"Shit, red man. I don't have a damn clue what you're

talking about. But as long as you keep payin' my salary,
I'll kick down as many doors as you want."

"Good," Grayfeather said as he turned a corner. "Now
let's see how our decoys are doing."

TWELVE

"Decoys?" Clint asked in a voice that got a little louder than he'd been planning.

Once he'd taken the guns away from the two men he'd chased into the boardinghouse, Clint didn't have any trouble at all convincing them to move their conversation through the back door of Rick's Place and into Hartman's private office.

Clint stood at the door leading to the outside, while Hartman himself stood at the door leading into the saloon's main room, cradling a shotgun in the crook of his arm. As for the two prisoners, they didn't seem too eager to go anywhere . . . especially since they were tied securely to their chairs by ropes circling them from their ankles all the way up to their shoulders.

"Did you say you were decoys?" Clint asked again in a slightly more subdued tone.

So far, only one of the men had been doing any talking. But with the amount of information that had been coming out of that one's mouth, he more than made up for the one who remained silent.

"Yeah," the talkative one said. "All we was supposed to do was keep you busy for the night. Make sure you didn't go anywhere unless we raised such a ruckus that it would be heard all over town."

Clint shook his head while glaring down at the bound figure. "I don't buy it. Who would hire you to do such a thing?"

"I swear I don't know."

Hartman had helped tie the men up, and had been watching Clint question them ever since. He stepped in closer to the silent prisoner and stuck his face within inches of that one's nose. "What about you?" he asked menacingly. "You don't seem to have a lot to say. I think that's because you know more than your friend."

The second figure looked up at Hartman without showing any trace of fear. In response to the saloon owner's question, he merely stared into Hartman's face and clenched his jaw shut even tighter.

"I think you should spend some more time with this one, Clint," Hartman said.

Clint turned so he could face Hartman, and took a moment to notice the way his friend was perched on the balls of his feet as though he was about to throw himself at the man tied to the chair in front of him. "And I think you're enjoying yourself a little too much here," Clint said.

Stepping away from the prisoners, Clint pulled Hartman with him by the sleeve of his shirt. He lowered his voice so that his words couldn't be heard by the men in the chairs. "What the hell's wrong with you? I thought I told you to give me some time alone back here. You actually look like you're having fun with this."

"You're damn right I'm enjoying myself. Men like these shoot up my bar every chance they get. It feels good to see them sweating for a change."

"Well, in case you haven't noticed, what we're doing isn't exactly legal. If they don't say anything real soon, we're gonna have to let them go."

Hartman's expression showed some genuine disappointment. "What? Why?"

"Just spare me the theatrics and keep an eye on them to make sure they don't try anything violent. Let me ask the questions, and then you're going to bring the sheriff in here to take them away."

"Fine," Hartman grunted. "But I still say we should—"

Clint silenced him with a quick wave of his hand. "No more from you. Just keep quiet and watch them."

Without waiting for another response, Clint turned his attention back to the two men inside the ropes. Walking over to them, he made sure to let his hand drop onto the handle of his Colt and stay there like a deadly, unspoken promise. "How about we cut through all the bullshit. I don't appreciate chasing after the likes of you all over town. Now you tell me everything about why you drug me away from a perfectly good card game and I won't let my anxious friend over there near you with an ax handle."

Defiance flashed in both of the prisoners' eyes, but it was merely a reflex. When Clint didn't blink at their mocking smiles, the men looked over at the saloon's owner.

"There's nothing like a nice piece of hickory," Hartman said while reaching for something behind a stack of liquor boxes.

Clint knew what was going through the other men's minds, and he only hoped that neither one of them had heard too much of what he'd just been saying to Hartman in the corner. The talkative one glanced over at his partner, receiving only a reluctant shrug for his trouble.

"I swear to God, I don't know the man's name," the prisoner said. "He was a big Injun with bones in his hair."

"Bones in his hair?" Clint asked.

"Yeah. He knew you'd be around town and just wanted

DEAD MAN'S EYES

us to make sure that you stayed put while he went about his business."

"And what business is that?"

"You got me. His money was reason enough for us to do it. We was going to walk inside this place and start shooting just to draw you out, but when I saw you watching us, I figured I could keep you busy just by acting suspicious. You came out after us just when I was gonna—"

"We weren't supposed to kill you," the second one said. Judging by the tone in his voice, that very point was something that had been stuck in his craw for some time. And when he glared over at his partner, it was obvious who was the true target of his anger. "I told you that a hundred times, Will. He guards this place like a dog, and all we had to do was sit out there and keep him watching us, but you had to start a fight."

Clint stepped between the two before they started tearing into each other. "So how did this Indian know I would be here?"

Both men looked at Clint as though he'd grown a set of horns.

"Everybody knows you're here," the talkative one stated.

Clint turned to look over his shoulder at Hartman. The saloon owner looked back with an amused expression, shrugged, and nodded his head.

THIRTEEN

"Great," Clint sighed. "It's nice to see that I'm so popular." Looking back at the talkative prisoner, he said, "You're going to be in a jail cell within the hour. You did your job, but it's safe to say that that means the Indian has done his as well. And since I'm pretty sure he won't be anxious to get too close to the law, it's also safe to say that he won't be walking into the sheriff's office to pay you any bonuses for the extra trouble you got yourselves into."

"He paid us already," the talkative one said with a smug grin.

"Which means he's already written you off." Leaning in closer to the man in the chair, Clint added, "And if he's done anything to hurt someone or . . . heaven forbid . . . kill someone, you two will be the only ones around to take the blame."

Gambling that he might strike a nerve with the direction he'd decided to take, Clint watched the man in front of him to see if his gamble might have paid off. In reality, he knew that the sheriff would be around any minute to collect the two prisoners, and that if he was going to get anything more out of them, it would have to be now.

For a couple seconds, there was only silence in the storage room. Then that silence was broken.

"Whatever it was that was supposed to happen," said the one who'd been content to say next to nothing this entire time, "it was supposed to be happening at a run-down hotel a couple blocks away."

"What the hell . . ." the first prisoner grunted.

"He's right," the quiet one replied. "We didn't get paid enough to get tossed in a cell. Even if it is for a night or two." Turning back to Clint, he added, "He's after some-body, but he didn't have any reason to tell us who it was."

Clint studied both men for the better part of a minute. The fact that they'd shot at him wasn't too big of a sur-prise since that seemed to be on the minds of just about any ambitious soul trying to make a living with his gun. And since the rest of their story seemed to check out with what they'd told him, he decided to end his discussion.

"Good enough," he said. "You two just sit tight and we'll fetch you when the sheriff gets here." Motioning for Hartman to follow, Clint opened the door and left the prisoners to bicker amongst themselves.

"So that's it?" Hartman asked as they headed for the bar.

"That was a lot more than I thought I'd get."

"What about this Indian? Whatever he was doing didn't sound too good. What about who he was after?"

Clint leaned over the bar and helped himself to a beer. "Whatever it is, it's over by now. The quickest way for us to find out will be to ask the sheriff when he gets here. When did you send for him anyway?"

"One of the kids who cleans up the place went for him as soon as we got them two situated. But don't try to change the subject, Clint. What are you going to do about all of this?"

After taking a mug from beneath the bar and filling it up at one of the taps, Clint took a sip and looked at Hart-

man. "Aren't you always the one telling me to relax and
let folks handle their own problems?"

"Yes, but—"

"Then take some of your own advice and let me relax."

Hartman's face nearly dropped to the floor. His jaw
hung open limply for a second or two while his brain
frantically searched for what he should say to that.

Clint let him sweat for a couple more seconds before
setting his beer on the bar and letting him off the hook.
"First of all, I'm not about to let all of this happen without
looking into it. Jesus, you've known me this long and you
really think I'd let something like this go by?"

Letting out a relieved breath, Hartman leaned his elbows on top of the bar. "You had me going there for a
second."

"It's too easy, friend," Clint said with a smile. "I've
been poking my nose into things like this for too long to
go out half-cocked based on the word of someone like
those two hog-tied in your storeroom. This town has too
many run-down hotels for me to know exactly where I
should go first. The sheriff will know something to point
me in the right direction.

"Once I know where to go, I'll head over there to make
sure someone isn't getting hunted down by this Indian
they were talking about."

"You think there's really an Indian?" Hartman asked.

"If not an Indian, there's somebody who paid them to
divert my attention. If not, they did a piss-poor job of
trying to kill me. Besides," Clint added, "I wasn't about
to believe them until that quiet one spoke up. He was too
angry to be lying so well. There's definitely something
going on here and I aim to find out what it is."

Hartman was about to say something else when his
head snapped toward the front door. If he'd been a dog,
his ears would have perked up in reaction to what he saw.
"Good. The sheriff just walked in. Looks like we've

learned something from all of this. You're just not cut out to relax for more than a few days at a stretch."

"Yep," Clint said after taking another sip of beer. "Unfortunately, I've also learned that me being here is common knowledge to any shooter with their ear to the ground."

Nodding slowly, Hartman felt a dark mood come over himself and his longtime friend. "Sorry about that," he said regretfully. "I hope I didn't have anything to do with it. I mean, you're not exactly an easy man to hide."

"I know," Clint said. "Actually, there's been a part of me that's seen this coming for some time now. That's probably what's been setting my nerves on edge the last few days."

Despite the situation, Hartman had to laugh. "You know, when I saw you take off after them two outside this place, I swore there was something in your eyes that's been missing for some time. Most people get it when they have a long streak of luck at cards or if they get ahold of the right woman, but not you. I only see that look in your eyes when you know you're charging into the thick of things."

"As much as I hate to admit it, I think you're right about that. I guess a man can only live so long with the sky falling down around his ears before it gets hard to be happy when the pieces stop hitting my hat."

FOURTEEN

The sheriff made his way through the crowded saloon and over to where Clint and Hartman were standing. After only a few exchanged words, the lawman took a peek in the storage room and headed straight for the front door.

"I recognize 'em, all right," the sheriff said. "Heard they messed up Miss Langley's boardinghouse across the street."

"Nothing too bad," Clint replied. "But there might be more to it than that."

"Really?"

"Has anything else been happening around here tonight? Maybe in another part of town?"

The sheriff looked over his shoulder and signaled for a couple of his deputies to head into the storage room. "There was a scuffle at a hotel across from the Lucky Queen. Man got shot and a couple others chased some poor girl clean out of the place. Folks tell me she didn't even bother getting dressed before hightailing it out of there."

Nodding to himself, Clint said, "Sounds about right."

"I wasn't able to catch any sign of those killers," the sheriff said. "All I got to go on is the word of a few

58

witnesses who heard shots or saw a pair of men chasing the naked woman. Is there something else you'd like to tell me?"

Although Clint never had a problem working with the law, there was something about what was going on that night that didn't sit too well with him. It wasn't as though he wanted to hide anything from the sheriff, but he also didn't want to let too much out at this particular time either.

"Maybe," Clint said after a second or two. "Those two in the back know something about it, though. I talked to them until you showed up, but maybe they'll have more to say to you."

The sheriff looked like he wanted to press for more information, but the crow's-feet around his eyes as well as the bags beneath them spoke volumes about how he'd been running himself ragged over the last couple of hours. Shaking his head, he turned toward the storeroom just as three of his deputies were leading the prisoners out.

Both of the gunmen Clint had captured were still brushing off strands of freshly cut rope and rubbing sore spots on their wrists and shoulders. As they walked by, they turned defeated eyes toward the floor.

"You hear anything, Adams, you be sure to let me know," the sheriff said.

"Of course."

And since there didn't seem to be anything else to say, the lawman led his small parade out the door, much to the amusement of most of the people in the room, who stood by watching the procession as if it was the evening's entertainment. The moment the door slammed shut behind the last of the deputies, every conversation in the place picked up right where it had left off. Even the piano player resumed on the very note where he'd stopped.

Likewise, as Hartman signaled for the bartender to refresh their drinks, he looked at Clint and picked up where he'd left off before the lawman had shown up. "So I guess you'll be heading back into the thick of things, huh?"

"Looks like it. The sheriff looked like he had his hands full, and whatever happened at that hotel has already happened, so I can at least finish my drink."

"Don't blow smoke at me, Clint," Hartman said with a knowing grin. "You know just as well as I do that you're dying to head over there and see what happened. Hell, you won't let yourself rest until you've cleared this up and seen it through to the end."

"I'm that predictable, huh?"

"Yep," Hartman said while tipping back the rest of his beer. "And let's not forget old as well."

Clint stepped away from the bar and shot a warning glance toward the saloon's owner. "Don't push it, friend."

As much as he wanted to think otherwise, Clint knew for a fact that everything Hartman had said about him had been true. Despite all the times he'd thought about how great it would be to find a home and settle there, Clint couldn't deny the fact that there was something undeniably tugging him toward the mystery of what was going on in Labyrinth.

It wasn't a problem that would devastate the entire town. It probably wasn't much more than a jealous husband, or even a customer of the naked woman who would rather chase her into the street than pay what he owed her. The dead man could very well be some slimy bastard who'd simply gotten what was coming to him.

The truth, however, was that none of that mattered to Clint Adams. A mystery was a mystery, and he couldn't just stand by knowing that a killer was running free right outside his door.

That, quite simply, was the way he lived.

Clint might want to settle down somewhere like a normal man, but he'd lived too far outside the norm for too damn long. And what it all boiled down to was that was the way he liked it.

Coming to that realization was something of a victory inside Clint's mind. That one part of him that hadn't been letting him rest easy for the past couple of days was finally put to rest. And although he was sure he'd be hearing those same complaints coming from that part of himself, it sure felt good to be rid of them for the time being.

Still, along with that, there came another realization that wasn't so easy to bear. Rather than push it aside as he had with the rest, Clint looked back at Hartman and extended his hand. "Thanks," he said. "As always."

"Your money's never good in here, Clint," Hartman replied. "That's what friends are for."

"I'm not talking about the drinks. I'm talking about everything else. You're a good friend. Thanks for that."

Hartman nodded as he realized what was going on. He shook Clint's hand and said, "Anytime."

"After the last couple shooters came through here a while ago, I'd hate to bring any more your way. Especially since they all know exactly where to look for me."

"No problem. So I guess you'll be headed out of town for a while?"

"Yeah. When things cool down, I'll be back soon enough."

"You know where to find me."

Turning away from Hartman, Clint walked out of Rick's Place and headed toward the Lucky Queen Poker Hall. He knew he'd be headed out of Labyrinth soon after that.

FIFTEEN

After her blood stopped pushing through her veins at the speed of a runaway train, Emma started feeling the cool night air nibbling at the edges of her body. The tips of her fingers were starting to tingle and both of her feet were going numb.

She didn't know exactly how long she'd been running, but the crackling of gunfire she'd been using to guide her had quieted down long ago. For the moment, she sat at the back of a building that she guessed to be on another side of town from where she'd started. She'd been sure to put plenty of distance between herself and her pursuers, while staying close enough that they might just go past her while hunting her down.

When she closed her eyes, Emma could see the dirty floor pressed against her cheek and could smell the stench of Darryl's blood and bodily fluids as they'd soaked through the mattress over her head. Although she hadn't gotten much more than a fleeting glimpse of the two men who'd killed her lover, she'd seen enough to tell her that they were the same men who'd been forcing her to move from town to town like some kind of gypsy for the last two years.

Well, one of them was the same anyway. She knew that much for certain.

After all, it wasn't easy to forget footsteps that had been pounding after you for so many nights in a row. Every so often, no matter how safe she thought she might be or how far she'd been running, Emma woke up with a start, certain that the thumping inside her chest was that giant Sioux marching toward her.

Sometimes, at times like these, she felt a little less frightened. When she knew for a fact that the Indian was coming after her, there was nothing else to be frightened of. There wasn't that nagging worry in the back of her mind that she might not be safe.

She knew she wasn't safe.

She knew he was out there.

And she knew he'd be coming for her.

Thoughts like those were what had filled the last hour or two. They kept her quiet whenever she heard someone passing by the alley on either side, and made it easier for her to wait for that inevitable moment when she would have to come out of her hiding place and face the horrors of the outside world one more time.

Emma took a deep breath, let it out, and opened her eyes. She sat beneath a set of dusty stairs leading up to the second floor of a tall, narrow building. The steps cut the sky above her into several skinny rectangles, making it so that she could only see part of her surroundings at any given time.

She liked that. It made her feel as though she didn't have to deal with everything that was going on at once. Pressing her back against the wall, she brought her knees in a little tighter against her chest and waited to hear those familiar footsteps come pounding toward her.

There were plenty of sounds filling the night air. Voices, laughter, shouting, dogs barking, crickets, even music. But no footsteps. Emma knew better than to let

herself take any comfort from that fact, but she did let
herself draw some strength from the notion that she'd
managed to slip away from within the Indian's closed fist.

Tears started crawling out of the corner of her eyes,
making cool little trails down her face as they trickled
over her skin to land upon the curve of her bottom lip.

Darryl was dead.

She'd only known him for a short time, but she'd somehow gotten attached to him. She'd allowed him to get
inside her heart and give her hope, but more than that,
she'd also gotten him killed.

Darryl would have still been alive if not for her. If it
wasn't for Emma, that Indian wouldn't have anything to
chase all the way across the country. If not for her, Darryl
would still be alive . . . along with the others.

Wiping away the tears with the back of her hand,
Emma forced herself to take another deep breath. This
time, she held it until her heart started to flutter inside her
chest and the blood shot beneath her skin like a desperate
little river inside her.

Emma reached out to grab hold of the step directly
above and in front of her. Using the solid wooden plank
as a support, she pulled herself up so she could get her
legs beneath her and support herself on the balls of her
feet. Every muscle below her waist cried out in pain as
she tried to shuffle out from under the stairs while lifting
her feet high enough to keep from making too much noise
in the process.

After what seemed like an eternity of scraping painfully
in the dirt, she could straighten up to her full height and
look at the stars above without anything else between herself and the heavens. The moon was just over halfway
there, but it seemed to shine down on her like a pale
version of the sun.

She wasn't familiar with the town, but had seen enough
of it to have a rough idea of where she was inside it.

Making her way slowly down the alley, Emma got her bearings while trying to pull herself together in the process. By the time she emerged from the end of the alley, she'd somehow managed to stop the tears from flowing and put on a reasonably normal expression.

It was dark enough for the people walking by not to notice that she wore no shoes on her feet. And as long as she kept moving, Emma was able to hold herself so that the dress actually looked as though it might have been somewhat close to her size.

She'd come to Labyrinth for a reason, after all.

And just because of what had happened to . . .

Just thinking about the last couple of hours was almost enough to bring the tears back. Even the faintest memory of Darryl's face or what had happened to him would have been more than enough to shatter the facade of normalcy that she'd constructed around her.

So she did the only thing she could at that particular moment and prevented herself from thinking about it. At least for now anyway.

She'd come to Labyrinth for a reason.

And just because of what had happened, she wasn't about to abandon that reason along with the only, faint glimmer of hope that was left in her world.

Darryl had . . .

No, she thought to herself. Don't think about him.

She'd been told that she could find help in this town. She'd been told by a good friend that there was someone here who might be able to face someone like the Sioux who'd been given the task of hunting her down and snuffing out her life like a pair of fingers closing in around the tip of a candle.

Hopefully, that friend of hers hadn't been just as desperate as she was. Emma knew only too well that being desperate caused a person to cling to even the weakest branch as though it could support the weight of an entire family. Because if this wasn't a certain thing . . . if her friend hadn't been completely right in what he'd told her, Emma wasn't sure if she'd be able to run much longer.

She held her head up and walked as close to the edge of the boardwalk as she could without making it too obvious that she was trying to remain in the shadows. Only one thing kept her from breaking down again. Only one thing kept her moving down the same streets that were being used by the men whose job it was to kill her.

Clint Adams was there. He was somewhere in Labyrinth.

He had to be.

SIXTEEN

As far as Clint could tell, if there was anything else going on in Labyrinth besides what had happened at Rick's Place, he was nowhere near it. Walking at a brisk pace down the street to the Lucky Queen, he couldn't find much more than the usual traffic of locals and strangers making their way from saloon to saloon and brothel to brothel.

Not that he doubted the sheriff's word, but it wasn't hard to see that he'd missed whatever action had taken place in this part of town. Even the faces he passed seemed perfectly at ease with the cool, quiet hue the night had taken on. By the time Clint reached the poker hall, even he was somewhat more relaxed than when he'd set out from Hartman's saloon.

The Lucky Queen wasn't one of the nicer places to play cards in Labyrinth, but that didn't keep it from being one of the most popular. It wasn't as big as Rick's Place, and didn't even provide much else besides a bunch of tables and a bar. Still, it was within stumbling distance of no fewer than half a dozen bordellos and at least three fairly comfortable places to sleep for the night. As soon as the sun went down, the poker hall was nearly filled to capacity with games ranging from one end of the high-stakes spectrum to the other. Clint had played there a few times himself. That is, whenever he couldn't find an empty chair at Rick's.

Stepping onto the boardwalk, Clint looked across the street at the Lucky Queen and studied the place for a few seconds. He then turned around to look at the building directly behind him. It wasn't much bigger than a two-family home, and the only thing separating it from a private residence was the "Rooms for Rent" sign hanging over the front door.

Half of the windows had a warm, flickering glow behind them. The door swung open easily with a single push, and the moment Clint stepped inside, he was looking straight down the barrel of a raised shotgun.

"That's far enough, mister," came a harsh, trembling voice. "Get your hands away from that gun and get the hell out. I've had enough trouble for one night."

Clint lifted his arms over his head and took a step back. "Whoever it is you're expecting," he said carefully, "I'm pretty sure it's not me."

"Better let me be the judge of that."

The voice from behind the shotgun came from an old lady who looked as though she'd been chewed up and spat out . . . several times. Her skin had the texture of badly tanned leather, and was stretched over her bones like a tepee that clung to its stick frame after years of improper treatment. What little hair she had was bunched up inside a simple bonnet that had been hastily thrown on top of her head.

Any indications of frailty ended there, however. Her hands gripped the shotgun tightly without wavering the slightest bit. Although her back was stooped, she looked as though a gale-force wind couldn't knock her over and her eyes regarded Clint with the clarity of a hawk.

"You can leave now," she said simply.

"I don't think you understand. All I want is—"

The shotgun jutted forward another inch or so as both hammers were snapped back. "I think it's you that don't understand. I said for you to leave and that's what you should do. I already had a shootin' in here tonight. Another one won't make much difference."

"That's why I'm here," Clint said. "I wanted to ask you about that shooting."

The old woman's face lost a little of its tension. Not much, but a little. "You with the sheriff?"

"No, ma'am. I just wanted to see if there was anything I could do to help. If there's anything you might know about what happened, I'd sure like to hear it. But if you want me to leave, I'll respect your wishes."

"Well, well, well. Ain't that just right neighborly of you? Say . . . have I seen you around here before?"

"Could be. I'm—"

"You're that Adams fella."

"That's right. You can call me Clint if you'd prefer."

Slowly, the shotgun came down from the woman's shoulder and was lowered to hang at her side. She raised an empty right hand and when Clint took it, he was surprised by the strength that was behind those gnarled, knobby fingers.

"I heard'a you," the woman said. "Even had a few of my guests say that it was you that killed that poor fella upstairs. But that's just because they only know you for your reputation. I set 'em straight, though."

"I appreciate it."

"Yep. I seen them two chase that poor girl down them stairs. She was so scared that she didn't even bother covering herself up. Can't say as I blame her, since I also got a look at them two once they decided to stroll out after her."

Sensing the change in the woman's mood, Clint let his hands come down and took a few steps inside the front

room. The place was decorated much like someone's
house, complete with family photographs on the wall and
lace doilies beneath empty glass vases.

"So there were two of them?" Clint asked.

"Yessir. And I knew neither could be you because one
of them was too small and . . . not half as handsome as I
heard you were."

"And the other?"

"He was an Injun. Big one too. Looked like he had the
first man on kind of a short leash. Kept telling him to
quiet down and not be in such a rush. Even mistook him
for one of the other guests on account of how calm he
was. Plus my eyes ain't quite what they used to be. That's
why I was so quick to point this old thing at you when
you walked through the door," she said while propping
the shotgun up against a large desk. That desk was the
only thing in the room distinguishing it from the parlor
of any other family's home.

"Do you know who was killed?"

The old woman walked around to the other side of the
desk, nodding as though she already knew the question
was on its way. "He signed the register when he paid for
the room just the other night. Him and that woman of his
didn't come out of that room 'cept to take in their meals.
I thought they was newlyweds."

Squinting down at the pages, she turned up a nearby
lamp and waved Clint over. "Here it is. See for yourself."

Clint walked up to the desk as the woman turned the
register around so he could read it. The two pages he
could see went all the way back over the past three days,
with several of the entries marked with hastily scribbled,
illegible lines or even the occasional X. The woman
pointed to one in particular, written in a blocky, masculine
script.

"Darryl and Mrs. Besskin?" Clint said, reading the sig-
nature out loud.

"That's what they went by. But if you ask me, I'd say there was something wrong about them."

The more he looked at the old woman, the more Clint was certain there was a whole lot more going on inside her that didn't show up on the surface. "Really?" he asked. "How so?"

"I didn't see much of them besides mealtimes, but the woman seemed awful skittish. She liked her man well enough, but there was a couple times she didn't seem too comfortable answering to the name she gave me."

"Like you said . . . she could be a newlywed."

"True enough," the old woman replied with a shrug. "But most girls that age are proud to wear their new names. She seemed to be nervous about something. Maybe even scared."

Clint nodded along with her and glanced down at the shotgun, which rested well within her reach. Although the old woman looked like she'd seen more than her share of hard times and was obviously no stranger to violence, it was plain to see that Mrs. Besskin wasn't the only scared woman in this town.

SEVENTEEN

"Mind if I look at their room?"

"It ain't pretty." Looking around while leaning forward, the old woman lowered her voice to a whisper. "The undertaker ain't been around yet to collect the body. If it's all the same to you, I'd appreciate it if you didn't let any of my other guests see what's in there. Bad for business and all."

Before heading up the stairs, Clint smiled warmly at the woman behind the desk and said, "You notice an awful lot, don't you?"

"It pays for a girl to keep her eyes open. Especially when she's in a position to see things that might help other folks."

"Do you know who chased Mrs. Besskin down the stairs?"

"Actually, she wasn't really chased. I told the sheriff that and he didn't want to hear much else about them."

"But did you get a look at their faces? Did you maybe recognize one of them?"

"No, sir," she said while her eyes twitched down toward her folded hands. "I told you what I saw. And the only reason I told so much was because I know who you

are and I know you'd only be trying to help that poor girl
being hunted down by those animals."

Clint was struck by the old woman's particular choice
of words. But by the look on her face, she was becoming
extremely uncomfortable with the turn the conversation
had taken. So, rather than push her any farther into unfriendly territory, he thanked her for what she'd given him
and checked the register once again for the Besskins'
room number.

On his way up the stairs, Clint thought about what he'd
been told about the woman running down those same
steps, naked and scared out of her wits. He looked down
at his feet while climbing to the second floor, spotting the
occasional dark stain on the wood.

All he had to do was scrape his boot over the smudge
to know that the dark wetness hadn't been there long
enough to dry. The stain was almost black and had the
thick, viscous texture that he'd become all too familiar
with over the years.

Blood.

It could have been a few other things, but deep in his
gut, Clint knew the substance staining the stairs was
blood. There wasn't much, and a lot of it had probably
been stepped on by the sheriff as well as the two men
who'd walked down after Mrs. Besskin after driving her
out in such a rush.

Since he wasn't exactly looking for proof that there'd
been a shooting, Clint walked over the spots of blood he
could see and made his way to the Besskins' room. The
upstairs hall was long and narrow, bordered on both sides
by doors that looked as though they would have been
more comfortable hanging on closets rather than anything
made to hold a bed and washbasin.

The hairs on the back of Clint's neck raised up as he
got close enough to the room for him to put his hand on
the knob. For a moment, Clint thought he could feel some

of the fear left over from when Mrs. Besskin had run out
through this door. That, added to the powerful smell of
blood and gunpowder, made Clint pause after twisting the
knob before pushing open the door.

When he finally did open the door, Clint took a quick
step inside as his hand reflexively went for the Colt at his
hip. There was still an acrid fog hanging near the ceiling,
which gave the room an eerie feel along with the smell
of burnt gunpowder.

Clint walked all the way into the room and closed the
door behind him as soon as he heard the sound of footsteps coming from the other end of the hall. The old
woman's request echoed through his brain as the steps
came down the hall, stopped in front of the door, and then
eventually moved on.

After turning up the lantern, which sat on a small table
along one wall, Clint looked down at the bloody remains
of Mr. Besskin. It didn't take a great mind to figure out
what had killed the man. After all, there was a hole in his
head big enough to fit a broomstick. What little furniture
there was in the cramped quarters was either knocked over
or sitting at awkward angles, as though the entire place
had been shaken by some giant trying to get the last nickel
from a cash register.

Since there wasn't much of anyplace to hide anything,
it only took Clint a minute or two to look at what else
the room had to offer. Besides what had probably been
there when the Besskins arrived, there were only enough
personal items to fit inside a single bag. And in the darkened corner farthest away from the lamp was that bag,
turned inside out and stomped flat.

Clint was just about to leave the room when he heard
something that caught his attention. At first, he thought it
might be a rodent scratching at one of the baseboards, but
the noise came from too high up to have been caused by
anything so close to the floor.

Suddenly aware of the noise he made just by breathing, Clint silenced even that for a few seconds as he waited to hear the sound again.

He stood there in the messy little room with the dead man staring up at him with three wide, gaping eyes. The more he looked at that man's body, the more Clint swore he saw parts of it start to move. Even though he knew that was just an illusion caused by the sputtering light falling over the corpse's eyelids and the curves of its face, Clint couldn't keep the chill from running through his flesh.

No matter how familiar he was with death, he wasn't immune to its icy touch.

Standing in that room, holding his breath as the stench of dried blood and other ripe bodily fluids assaulted his senses, Clint felt something cool and clammy seeping into the back of his mind. His eyes were drawn to the hole in the dead man's skull just as his hand was drawn to the modified Colt at his side.

Both things were connected, he knew. Cause and effect. It didn't matter which gun had drilled what hole. One thing led to another. Eventually, everyone in Clint's way got their turn staring through dead man's eyes.

It was only a matter of time.

Tak.

When the sound came again, it nearly caused Clint to jump in surprise. This time, it came from directly behind him at roughly neck level. He turned around, preparing himself to draw, despite the fact that common sense told him that wouldn't be necessary.

Tak.

Reaching out, Clint grabbed hold of the tattered, dirt-colored curtains and pulled them aside. The window behind them wasn't much bigger than his head and shoulders, but the glass in its pane was easily the cleanest thing in the room.

Clint was careful not to expose too much of himself as he peeked out the window and studied Third Street below. Besides an excellent view of the Lucky Queen's roof, there wasn't much to see besides the steady trickle of people walking in and out of the poker hall.

Tak.

This time, Clint was waiting for the sound. In fact, he even caught a glimpse of the pebble as it smacked against the outside of the window. Instincts bred through decades of sitting behind rifles and scopes of all kinds fed Clint angles and trajectories instantaneously, allowing him to pick a few spots on the street where that pebble might have come from.

Almost immediately, his eyes were drawn to one of those spots, which was occupied by a single, fragile figure staring intently back up at him. Still cautious, Clint allowed more of himself to be seen through the window as he gave the woman a single acknowledging wave. She waved back before stepping into the shadow of the building next to the Lucky Queen.

"Sorry to run off so quickly," Clint said to the unblinking man on the bed. "But I think I might have found your wife."

EIGHTEEN

Clint stepped out into the night after closing up the bloody room and saying his good-byes to the old woman guarding the front door. It felt real good to be outside after being cooped up with the stale stench of drying blood. The mixture of cool breezes, cigar smoke, and liquor permeated his senses, which were hungry to clean out what they'd been forced to take in only moments before.

Adjusting himself to the change of viewpoints, Clint thought back to what he'd seen from the upstairs window, and then found that same spot on the other side of the street. The woman wasn't where he'd last seen her, but that didn't surprise him too much since she'd had the air about her of a rabbit that was itching to bolt for another hiding place.

Clint walked across the street as though he was simply walking into the Lucky Queen. Once he was fairly certain that nobody else was paying him any mind, he turned away from the poker hall's entrance and headed for the neighboring building. He only had to walk a couple steps in that direction before he was greeted by the sight of a slender figure emerging from the shadows. Her arms were

wrapped around her upper body and her eyes stared out
at him with obvious fear.

Noticing the way she trembled, Clint removed his
jacket and held it out in both hands. "You look cold," he
said. "Why don't you put this on and we can talk."

The woman seemed hesitant at first, but she came forward in a few quick steps to snatch the jacket from Clint's
hand. She held the jacket and looked up at him.

"It's all right," he said. "I know it's not much, but
there's not much of a chill in the air."

Doing his best not to stare at her, Clint couldn't help
but notice the way the woman's clothing stuck to her
body. Her plain cotton dress wasn't more than a light-
colored slip, plastered to her skin by a layer of sweat from
the inside and dirt on the outside. As much as she tried
to cover herself, she was unable to hide the fact that she
wore nothing else beneath the flimsy material.

The moment she got Clint's jacket wrapped around herself, the woman allowed herself to stand up a little
straighter. Likewise, the trembling that had taken hold of
her limbs and torso tapered off to a subtle shiver.

"My name's Clint Adams. Are you Mrs. Besskin?"

The look on the woman's face was pure confusion at
first. Then, a shadow seemed to pass over her features
that forced her to look down at her bare feet. "That . . .
was Darryl's name. I told him to use another one, but
he'd already signed the book."

Clint looked around at the people walking along the
street. Although none of them seemed particularly interested in what he and the woman were doing, a few took
second glances at the visibly disoriented young woman.

"Come on," Clint said as he offered her his hand. "Let's
have a seat and talk about this somewhere inside. You
look like you could use something hot to eat." When he
didn't get so much as a look in response, Clint added, "Or
better yet . . . something stiff to drink."

Amazingly enough, that got something of a smile from the woman. She nodded weakly and took Clint's hand. When she saw that he was headed for the poker hall, she planted her feet and shook her head.

"No," she said in a fierce whisper. "Not here. It's too close to . . ."

Clint put his other arm around her shoulders and urged her forward. "I know, but you look like you've done more than enough running for one night. Besides," he added in a more intent tone, "this would be one of the last places anyone would look for you."

That, more than anything else, struck something inside the woman. She reluctantly started walking again, her steps becoming easier since Clint made an effort to keep himself positioned so that she didn't have to look at the boardinghouse across the street.

The moment he stepped inside, Clint could feel a difference in the woman by his side. As they were surrounded by the sounds of music and conversational voices as well as the smells of food and drink, the muscles in the woman's body started to relax. She felt like a frozen lump of clay thawing out inside his jacket until it was transformed into a normal human body.

Clint was sure to get a seat near the back of the room at one of the few tables not reserved for hosting card games. Unlike a saloon, the poker hall didn't waste any space on a stage, and only used the bare minimum for tables and a bar to service the needs of its gamblers. It wasn't hard to get swallowed up by the crowd and become just two more within the sea of those seated inside the large room.

"Keep your head down," Clint said in a way to keep from scaring the woman any further. He could see that she was starting to shrug his jacket off her shoulders, but Clint reached out to pull it back over her. "Better keep that on as well. As long as you sit with your back to the door, nobody will notice you unless you do something to attract attention. Just stay put and I'll be right back."

The young woman's face lit up with a sudden burst of fear. "No. Please don't leave me."

"It's all right," Clint said soothingly. "I'm just going to have some food sent over. I'll be watching you the whole time."

Walking over to the small hole in the wall that led to a sparse, yet functional kitchen, Clint knocked on the empty window frame until he got the cook's attention. Set up less for meals and more to simply quiet the cardplayers' stomachs between hands, the kitchen was only slightly bigger than something found in someone's house.

Clint placed an order for a plate of hot sandwiches and paid in advance, saying that he would be back in a few minutes to pick them up. Every so often, he glanced back at his table at the frightened woman who sat wrapped in his jacket, tensed as though she was waiting to join the man who was lying in her room.

NINETEEN

John Grayfeather walked the streets of Labyrinth, his eyes trained on a spot directly in front of him and his ears soaking up every sound that rode the breeze. He walked mostly to work the blood through his legs. Keeping his hands stuffed inside his pockets, the Indian strolled as though he didn't have a care in the world.

He strolled as though he wasn't wanted for murder by the lawmen walking those very same streets.

"I swear to God," Rhyne muttered. "This job would've been over a long time ago if you didn't insist on coming along every damn step of the way."

Until the other man had actually spoken, Grayfeather had all but forgotten the gunman was still there. Blinking a couple times in quick succession, he turned his head to look Rhyne in the face. "What did you say?"

"I said . . . aw, never mind. Should we even keep lookin' for that whore or are we giving up?"

"We're a long way from giving up, Mr. Rhyne. We just missed an opportunity, that's all. There will be others."

"Sure," the gunman sneered. "And them others will die just like that one up in that room back there."

"That wasn't your doing."

"The hell it wasn't!" Catching himself as his voice raised into an angry pitch, Rhyne stopped where he was and took a deep, growling breath. "If you want me to kill these men, I couldn't give a damn. All I want to know is why. What's that girl to you?"

Grayfeather shook his head. He could see those words coming as though they'd been written on a piece of ground that he slept on every night. Although he knew the killer was just a simple man looking for explanations, that didn't make it any easier for the Sioux to put up with him. Especially at trying times like these.

Rather than answer Rhyne's question or any of the questions that were sure to follow, Grayfeather lifted his nose to the fresh, clean air and kept walking.

Finally, once the noise beside him came to a stop, the Sioux rounded a corner and looked at Rhyne. "We'll continue this hunt tomorrow," Grayfeather said. "Get some sleep and be ready to move out after first light."

"Fine." Wearing a look on his face as though he'd smelled something bad, Rhyne thrust his hand out and put the other on the handle of his gun. "I'll take my next week's salary in advance."

Finally, Grayfeather seemed interested in something the other man had to say. At the very least, if he wasn't interested, he was most certainly amused. "You will? And why is that?"

"Because a man like me don't appreciate getting jerked around at the end of a leash by no Injun. If you want to waste my time, that's your choice, but you got to pay for the privilege."

Grayfeather looked down at the gunman as though he was observing a particularly interesting insect. He knew it could buzz anywhere it wanted, just as he knew it could sting him if provoked the wrong way. But none of that bothered the Sioux too much. On the contrary, it brought the faint prelude of a smile to the corners of his mouth.

Both of Grayfeather's hands moved in a simultaneous blur. In the darkness, the movement could have easily been mistaken as a trick of the shadows. As a result, Rhyne barely knew whether he should react until the motions were already complete and the big Sioux was once again a picture of total calm.

When Rhyne realized that Grayfeather had indeed moved so quickly, his initial response was to move his hand down toward his holster. As he did, the money that had been placed in his open palm fell to the ground and several of the silver dollars bounced off the top of his boot.

"There's the money that's so important to you," Grayfeather said. "Be sure to take real good care of it while you still can."

"What the hell's wrong with you damned Injuns?" Rhyne blustered, even as his hand clamped uselessly around the butt of his gun. "I swear to God above that you ain't good for nothin' but—"

"Oh, and one more thing," the Sioux interrupted. "If you call me an Injun once again, I won't be so slow with my other hand."

Rhyne stared back at Grayfeather with a completely blank expression. Then, when he saw the smile creep over the bigger man's features, he felt the gentle poke of something sharp and metallic against his midsection. When he looked down, Rhyne saw the blade being pressed against his underbelly, the knife clutched in Grayfeather's other hand. Rhyne started to say something else, but was silenced by another prod from the knife. This time, the tip managed to slide through the material of his shirt.

"No hard feelings, John," Rhyne said with a sugary smile on his face. "After all, I was just griping. That's all. Didn't mean nothin' by it."

Grayfeather nodded slowly, twisting the blade a little before withdrawing it and slipping back into the sheath hidden beneath his tunic. "That's what I thought. But if it's all the same to you, I'd still prefer it if you kept a more civil tone when talking to me."

"Sure, sure."

"And the girl as well."

"Huh?"

"Don't call her a whore."

Every time Rhyne saw the Indian's reaction to the woman they were chasing, a new set of assumptions sprung up inside his mind. Now was no different, but he knew better than to voice any of them out loud. "My mistake," he said through that same shit-eating grin.

Grayfeather didn't think for one moment that anything the gunman was saying was sincere in the least. But on the other hand, he knew for damn sure that he wasn't going to have to hear those vulgarities coming out of Rhyne's mouth anytime soon.

"Good," Grayfeather said as his empty hands were crossed over his chest. "Tomorrow the hunt starts again. Be ready for it." And with that, Grayfeather turned and headed back to the room he'd rented on the other side of town.

"I'll be ready," Rhyne said as he started walking in the opposite direction. "More ready than you'd ever guess."

TWENTY

The sandwiches provided by the Lucky Queen weren't anything special. In fact, they were only a few sparse cuts of beef and ham slapped on day-old bread, but they still tasted awful good when washed down with the house beer. As soon as Clint set the food down in front of the woman sharing his table, he took one sandwich for himself and had a few bites. When he looked down again, the woman was already finishing the first sandwich of her own portion.

"At least your appetite's not suffering," Clint said. "Mind if I get another one of these, or will I be pulling back fewer fingers than when I started?"

The woman laughed and blushed a bit, which made her look like someone else entirely.

"Guess I left my manners somewhere else," she said. "Sorry about that."

Clint waved off the apology as if he was swatting a fly. "Forget it. Have as much as you want. You've been through a lot tonight."

"Yes," she said quietly as a dark mood came over her. "Yes, I have."

Clint let her eat the rest of her meal in silence. As she

filled her belly, she seemed to once again find the strength to push aside the darkness that was reflected in her eyes like a ghostly image looking out from behind green-tinted glass.

All the while, Clint kept his eyes on the front door, looking for anything suspicious or any faces that were turned in their direction one time too many. As far as he could tell, however, everyone else in the poker hall was concentrating too heavily on their cards to even know that Clint and his frightened guest existed. Even though he knew that the two men from the front of Rick's Place were tucked safely away by now, there was a part of Clint's mind that half expected to see them skulking about the front door of this place as well.

The woman's shoulder raised up and dropped down again as she let out a deep breath. Once she'd replenished the air in her lungs, she looked up at Clint and asked, "How did you know?"

"Know what?"

"What happened. About . . . what happened to Darryl. How did you know to come and find me?"

"Let's just say that I met up with a few odd characters earlier tonight. Once I realized that they'd been hired for an even odder reason, I had to find out what was behind it all. So I asked around to see what other strange things had been going on tonight, and your hotel came up at the top of the list."

Although that was a greatly simplified version of what had happened, Clint's explanation seemed to be enough to satisfy the woman. She nodded slowly and ran her fingertip along the top edge of her cup before taking another tentative sip of the warm beer inside.

"Now it's your turn to answer a question," Clint said. "How'd you know I was going to be in your room?"

Without even looking up from her beer, she said, "I've

been trying to find you all night long. Well . . . at least since what happened to Darryl."

On any other night, that might have taken Clint somewhat off guard. But tonight, however, Clint was ready for just about anything. "So you know who I am?"

"Yes," she replied. Now she looked up. Her green eyes locked onto Clint's without any desperation or fear in them. Instead, there was only gratitude reflected in those beautiful emerald pools. "Thank you," she said, even though she didn't have to. "Thank you so much for helping me."

"I haven't done much so far besides give you something to eat."

"You took the time to listen to me and you helped me before you even knew who I was."

"Actually," Clint said, "I still don't really know who you are. The register at your hotel was signed under Mr. and Mrs. Besskin, but you've already said that that's not you name."

Some of the color flushed back into her cheeks, and she covered her face with her hands. "You must think I'm so stupid," she said. "Here I am after all this time and I'm still running around like a chicken with my head cut off. You'd think I would have been able to think straight by now."

Reaching across the table, she extended her hand, which was immediately taken by Clint. "My name is Emma Deerborne."

"Was Darryl to be you husband?"

"No. Not quite. If he was around to answer that question, he might have given a different answer, though." Already, she was starting to show less shock when she thought back to the dead man. In its place was fond remembrance as well as genuine affection.

"So who was he?"

"Darryl watched over me for a while. Actually, he'd

been looking out for my interests for some time. A lot more than any of the others."

"Talking to you is quite a treat," Clint said. "Every time I get you to answer a question, you manage to put three more on my mind in its place. I'm already starting to think it would have been better if I'd have just let you eat your sandwiches in peace."

Emma shook her head and shrugged. "Believe me, I know just how you feel. Every time I think I've got things figured out, they suddenly become more mixed up than they've ever been."

"Then start off with what happened to you tonight."

Clint brought the conversation back around to that subject on purpose. Mainly, he wanted to get another look at Emma's reaction, but he also wanted to see if she might contradict anything she'd said already. As much as he wanted to trust someone as pleasant and beautiful as her, he knew better than to let such things sway him into letting his guard down. After all, even the dumbest dog started to flinch when the same hand was raised one too many times.

Averting her eyes, Emma didn't seem as though she was trying to look any more sorrowful than she actually was. Even though it had only been a matter of minutes since she'd been about ready to cry over the mention of Darryl's name, she now seemed to have already gotten a handle on the situation.

That in itself told Clint a lot about how the woman was put together.

"Darryl and I came to Labyrinth only a couple days ago," she said. "We rode in and he started looking as soon as we got a place to stay and we were sure that nobody would know where we were."

"So somebody was after you?"

"Yes," she replied as something else clouded her features. This time, it was stark fear that tinted her eyes and even pinched at the edges of her mouth. "They've been after me for years."

"Just you?"

Emma nodded. "Darryl came along to try and protect me, but he didn't know what he was up against. As many times as I tried to tell him, there was no way he could know. After a while, I stopped trying to warn him. I just wanted to get here . . . to Labyrinth. More than anything else in the world, I knew I had to get here. Once I did, I knew that I'd have a better chance of living to see another day."

Having gotten himself used to the fact that he would have to whittle away at her to get his answers, Clint was always ready with the next question to keep Emma talking. "Why did you have to get here so badly? What's in Labyrinth?"

Turning to look Clint straight in the eyes, Emma said, "You."

TWENTY-ONE

Now it was Clint's turn to be surprised.

"You came here for me?" he asked.

Emma flinched as though she was unsure whether or not she'd said the wrong thing. "It's nothing like that. Darryl brought me here because we knew that you've been living here. We just wanted to meet you and talk to you."

Clint's first reaction was to ask how she knew exactly where to find him. Then, Hartman's words echoed in his brain as though they'd been rattling around in there ever since the saloon owner had said them.

"Everyone knows," Hartman had told him.

Apparently, that was even truer than Clint could have realized.

"Well, now that you've got me all to yourself," Clint said while sitting back in his chair, "what is it you wanted to talk about?"

"I need your help . . . with those men that are after me."

"And why are they after you?"

That one question seemed to have an even bigger impact on Emma than the murder of the man who'd brought her into town. When she started to speak, the words caught in the back of her throat like fishhooks, bringing the appropriate painful grimace along with them.

"It started when I was only thirteen," she said. "I grew up in Dakota near the Badlands on Sioux territory. My father was an Indian and my mother ran away from her home in Massachusetts as soon as she was old enough. Growing up, I stayed with my father. It was hard, especially looking the way I did."

"You mean with the color of your skin?" Clint asked.

Emma nodded without any pain. Rather, she displayed a thick streak of pride that had probably been instilled within her ever since the bad names had started getting thrown at her. "Nothing too bad. Just a whole lot of remarks made by neighbors or insults heaped on top of a little girl whose hair was too light and skin wasn't dark enough. But my father made everything better. He always did."

While Emma talked, Clint kept looking toward the front door, expecting to see a shady figure looking back at any moment. For the time being, however, the world seemed to be going along just fine without giving him too much grief. Clint let himself enjoy the little respite, knowing it would probably be short-lived anyway.

Sitting just as she'd been told, Emma kept her head down and her back to the door. "When I turned eleven, a rumor got started about me. Some of the others who lived with me and my father started saying that the entire tribe was being punished for something my father had done. They said that I was the punishment sent to make the whole tribe pay for one man's mistakes."

Shaking his head, Clint thought back to all the times in the past that he'd been among the Indians. Just like any other group of people, they had their own mixture of good and bad members of the community. In fact, more often than not, the Indians seemed more willing to offer their help when it was needed than the white man. Clint could

even think of a few friends he'd made in the tribes scat-
tered throughout the country.

What he recalled the most was their simple, fundamen-
tal beliefs. They had their religions as well as their prac-
tices, but they weren't half as backward as they were
rumored to be. According to plenty of men, Indians
weren't anything more than savages who thought science
was nothing but magic.

Those were the kinds of Indians that would turn on one
of their own people's children. And those were the kinds
of Indians that Clint had learned existed primarily in the
tales of scalp hunters who made their living as killers for
the United States Cavalry.

"That doesn't sound like anything I've ever heard of,"
Clint said.

"Oh, really? And how many years did you live on tribal
lands?" Emma asked, her face tainted with genuine anger.
"Were you raised in the same place as me among all the
same people?"

"No, but it just sounds like one of the stories that get
started to stir up hate and suspicion in people's minds."

"That's ridiculous, Mr. Adams. The tribes are just as
different from one another as any other group of people.
They believe different things and act different ways.
Don't try to tell me about the people I grew up with unless
you were there."

Clint held her gaze, measuring her reaction against her
words. As far as he could tell, she wasn't trying to put
anything over on him just yet. In fact, she seemed about
one second away from getting up and storming out . . .
after tossing the rest of her drink into his face, of course.

"There's a lot of stories going around about your people, Miss Deerborne. I've heard that they kill babies and
cart away the bodies. I've heard that they've wiped out
entire towns from the face of the earth. Half of those
stories are exaggerations of things that happened decades

ago, and the other half are usually complete lies. I've learned to be extra careful when I'm told stories about the Indians. Usually, the one doing the telling is just trying to stir something up. Fear's a powerful weapon. Especially when mixed in with something that a lot of folks are already a little afraid of. So you'll just have to excuse me if I get a bit suspicious when someone starts talking about Indian curses and ghost stories."

Forcing herself to keep back the words she was about to say, Emma took a moment to calm herself. It didn't take her long, and when she was done, she seemed more at ease than ever. In fact, she was a completely different woman than the one that Clint had found outside the boardinghouse across the street.

"After living for so long with all of this, I get accustomed to having to defend my father as well as my people," she said. "Even after all of this, I still think of them as my people. If more people were like you, then there would be less around to believe those stories you were talking about. Thank you for that."

Clint was just as suspicious of words that were too kind as those that were too sharp. Even so, he said, "Just speaking my mind."

"To clear up what I was saying, the problem wasn't with whether or not the curse was true. The problem was that too many people believed it to be true."

"And who were they?"

"Folks within my own tribe . . . or . . . my father's tribe. They said they could feel the evil coming off of me. Called it bad medicine."

"And your father allowed this?" Clint asked.

"He didn't have any say in the matter. If he could, he would have been the first one to stand up for me. He would've taken on the whole tribe and moved heaven and hell to make sure nothing bad was said about his little girl."

"Then why didn't he?"

The corner of Emma's eye twitched. For a second, it looked as though there might have been something bothering her, like a piece of dust or even a gnat irritating her just beneath the lash. But then she dropped her face into her hands and let out a labored breath. That was when the teardrops started dripping from between her fingers, splashing onto the table below to form a small, salty pool.

"He didn't do any of those things for me because he was already dead by that time." Doing her best to wipe away as much of the moisture as she could, Emma lifted her chin and said, "He was the first man who died because of me. It was the curse. It killed him just as surely as if I would've put a gun to his head. It killed my father along with every other man I ever cared about. Just like it killed Darryl."

TWENTY-TWO

The hotel was one of the most luxurious in Labyrinth.
Although it would have surely paled when held up to a
bigger city's standards, the Texas Grand had some of the
softest beds to be found in all of West Texas. Even so,
the man who stayed in room number twelve had yet to
truly partake of his surroundings.

Sitting on the floor between his bed and a small writing
desk, John Grayfeather contemplated the hunt while looking at the stars through an open window framed by curtains of fine velvet. He imagined that he could feel his
spirit leaving his body, slipping through the glass pane,
and drifting lazily in the cool night air.

He allowed his spirit to be carried by the winds
wherever they might go. Up, down, in twisting little cy-
clones that played havoc with the stacks of newspapers
on the corner, none of that mattered. All that mattered
was that he could feel his own freedom.

That was the only thing that was truly important to him.
Freedom.

That he should be able to ride wherever he desired was
enough of a cause to fight, kill, and die for. He'd been
taught that the hard way while living within the fences

built by the white man. Staring out the window after traveling for so long by his own rules, Grayfeather felt freer than ever.

His mind drifted from such abstract pleasures to those of his more immediate concern: the hunt.

The hunt was about freedom as well.

The hunt was about freeing himself from the noose that had been placed around his neck and had been slowly tightening ever since. Just thinking about it was enough to rattle Grayfeather's tranquil rest. Like an eagle that had been shot while soaring through the sky, Grayfeather's spirit could no longer keep its place on top of the wind.

It came crashing down, slamming so hard back into the Sioux's body that when his eyes were torn away from the window, he swore he could hear glass breaking.

Grayfeather's peace could only come in small doses now. That was how it had been ever since he'd first felt the touch of that cursed woman's plague upon his soul.

She had a hold on him.

She always had and always would, until one of them was unable to draw another breath.

That was the problem with being cursed.

It was something that he could escape from every now and then, but it wasn't as though he was ever truly free. Through the blessings of his elders, Grayfeather was able to lead the hunt on behalf of the rest of the tribe, but that didn't make him a free man.

All it did was give him the illusion of freedom similar to the illusion of flight that he'd been feeling only moments before. It was enough to sustain him over short periods of time, but not enough to allow him to truly be considered one of the birds who lived in the air. That would only come once the witch who held onto his soul was dead.

Just like the eagle who waited for the wind and all the other elements to cooperate with him so it could swoop

in just the right way and slice the string that tied it to its
handler's arm, Grayfeather needed every single element
to be in his favor if he was going to lift the burden from
his own soul. He had to wait for this perfect combination
of circumstances if he was going to avoid the fate of all
the others that had been tainted by Emma Deerborne's
medicine.

Grayfeather knew why she'd come to this place. After
all, he wouldn't have been any kind of hunter if he wasn't
aware of what motivated his prey. He also knew that once
she'd gotten away from himself and Rhyne back at the
hotel, she would be ready to use any means at her disposal
to escape the trap she'd stumbled into.

And those means included cinching the noose around
Grayfeather's own neck just a little tighter. He could feel
that the moment his tomahawk had landed in the wall over
her head as she fled away from him. The only thing saving
his life was the fact that he'd let her go so she could feel
more secure, at least for the time being.

When he thought of that, Grayfeather smiled grimly to
himself.

She would never truly be secure again.

Even if it took him the rest of his days, Grayfeather
would be the shadow forever connected to her heels, always lingering just behind her until the time was right for
him to reach out and sever the bond connecting them.

One moment was all he needed. One clean strike to end
her life and reclaim his own. Only then would the curse
be lifted from himself as well as from the rest of his people.

Only then would he be truly free.

TWENTY-THREE

As he walked down the street, Douglas Rhyne made the same plans in the back of his mind as he had every other time he'd managed to get out from under Grayfeather's watchful eye. Those times were few and far between, but he was getting better at finding ways to separate from the Injun's side whenever possible.

It also helped that he'd learned exactly what the Sioux liked to hear so that Grayfeather would trust him more as a partner than as a hired hand. Rhyne had been attached to Grayfeather's side from the moment he'd been contacted by one of the other members of the Sioux's tribe. And though he didn't quite understand what made this "hunt" more special than any other bounty, he'd been more than happy to go along with it as long as the pay kept coming.

Some things, however, weren't worth any amount of pay. No matter how much money he got for the job, Rhyne was more than ready for this one to be over. He had his notions about how to end this particular period of employment. The only tricky part would be doing it so that he didn't wind up on the wrong side of a deal gone wrong.

The sheriff's office wasn't hard to find. When he'd passed it earlier in the day, Rhyne had made a mental note so he could retrace his steps when the time was right. Now that the time had come, he hurried to the small building and pushed open the door.

Some sense in the back of his mind put extra speed into his motions. His instincts sent a chill down his spine, as though the crazy Indian was right behind him, waiting with that tomahawk in hand.

"Something I can do for you?" the young man near a small desk asked.

Making sure the door was shut tightly behind him, Rhyne walked up to the desk so fast that the lawman behind it instinctively put his hand on top of his gun.

"Actually," Rhyne said, "there's something I can do for you. You're the sheriff?"

"No. He went home after completing his rounds, but I'm one of his deputies. What can I do for you?"

"I'd rather talk to the sheriff, but I ain't got the time to wait. There's a bounty I'll be dragging in here."

The deputy nodded as he realized what he was dealing with. "All right. If it's a legal bounty, you'll get your money."

"You don't understand. I need someone to help me. This bounty ain't about to come in too quietly."

"They usually don't," the deputy remarked with a wry smile. "That's why there's professionals out there to bring them in. Maybe you should talk to one of them instead of me. And if you'd like some advice, I'd recommend that you stay away from too many dangerous men. At least until you get more experience in this line of work anyway."

Rhyne's fist came slamming down on top of the desk, rattling the pencils and bits of clutter that littered its surface. "Dammit, just listen to me for a second. He's the one that killed that man in the boardinghouse across from

the poker hall earlier tonight. And he's fixin' to hunt down
the girl that got away. When he catches up to her, he'll
kill her too. I just thought you might want to know."

The deputy's eyes widened as he jumped to his feet.
"Jesus! Are you sure about all of that?"

Nodding, Rhyne backed away to let the deputy charge
out from behind the desk. "I know where he is and if you
hurry, you should be able to take him without too much
of a fight. But I want something for bringing him in."

"If you're right about this, you'll get a reward for the
information. But first tell me where he's at. We'll take it
from there."

Rhyne gave the deputy a quick rundown on where
Grayfeather was staying. "Last I saw, he was in his room,
but I don't know how long he'll be there. You'd best
hurry if you want to catch him."

"Oh, we'll hurry. Now, you'll have to leave so we can
get on with this."

"What about my reward?"

"Come back tomorrow morning and talk to the sheriff."

Rhyne couldn't get in another word as he was pushed
out of the office by the deputy, who barked orders to a
few other younger men wearing similar badges on their
chests. Less than a minute later, the first deputy sprinted
out of the office and charged down the street.

After the deputy disappeared into the night, Rhyne
smiled to himself and started trotting toward the Texas
Grand. He couldn't have asked for that to go any better.
In fact, he'd even been hoping that the sheriff wouldn't
be in the office at that particular time, since that would
have only slowed things up that much more.

Youth combined with inexperience was a combination
that Rhyne loved in others. Especially when those others
were law. Bright-eyed deputies like the one he'd sent running made for perfect unwitting partners. Rhyne had
pulled this stunt several times in several other towns, and

it always started with some runt kid who was eager to please his boss.

It took no time at all for Rhyne to get back to the hotel where Grayfeather was staying. As he moved up the stairs toward the Indian's room, he tried to figure as best he could how long it would be before the sheriff came charging in to save the day.

After putting on his most convincingly worried expression, Rhyne stepped up to Grayfeather's door and started rapping on the polished wood. Within seconds, the door cracked open to reveal a dark sliver of the Sioux's face.

"What is it?" Grayfeather asked.

"It's the law. They're on their way over here."

The Sioux looked at him for a second or two before he stepped aside and opened the door enough for Rhyne to step inside.

"I told you we should've finished this job when we had a chance," Rhyne said as he entered the luxurious room.

"Why did this happen?"

"I don't know. Maybe someone told the sheriff after seeing us leave that boarding—"

"No," Grayfeather said as a gun appeared in his hand. "I mean, why did you pick this moment to turn against me?"

TWENTY-FOUR

Right when Clint thought he might have Emma Deerborne figured out, she would say something to completely throw him off again. First, she would seem like a victim doing her best to shake her pursuers, and then she would seem right as rain. One moment she would be grieving for her friend whose body was still lying in the room she'd shared with him, and then she would seem to be completely over the loss.

And in the midst of this confusion, Clint was starting to wonder if there really might be some bit of truth to this story of an Indian curse. Especially after what she'd just told him.

"You say this curse killed your father and Darryl?" Clint asked.

Emma nodded as though her head was suddenly too heavy to hold up anymore. "Yes."

"But I thought you said those killers shot Darryl."

"That's how the curse works. The men I'm with just . . . die. Sometimes it's disease, but usually it's . . . bloody. Like what happened to Darryl."

Suddenly, everything became a little clearer inside Clint's mind. At that moment, he felt silly for even starting to believe what Emma had been saying. "I see. Actually, I know what you're talking about here," Clint said as he reached out and put his hand over Emma's. "If folks tell you something too many times, you start to believe it. That can happen to anyone. In fact, I saw something like this down in New Orleans. This fellow had people convinced that he could come back from the dead—"

"No, Mr. Adams. My curse is real and I need you to help me lift it."

After talking with her for this long, Clint knew that it was useless to try to get any straight answers out of her when it came to this curse. But even though he didn't believe in curses, he believed that Emma Deerborne was definitely in a mess of trouble. And that was something he could do something about.

"What did you have in mind?" he asked.

"I need to get to a medicine man in Oklahoma. He can cleanse me and I can get back to my normal life. It's all I've been trying to do, but the man that's after me doesn't want me to get there."

"Why not?"

"Because he thinks I'll only bring my curse to another tribe and infect another group of people. He says I'll just kill more innocents just like I do wherever I go."

As she said that, Emma looked over her shoulder toward the front door. Her eyes lingered on the window facing the street, focusing on the boardinghouse opposite the Lucky Queen. Seeing the boardinghouse brought the sorrowful shadow back to her face, so she turned around to look at Clint.

"Whether you believe me or not about the medicine man, once I get to Oklahoma, there's friends there that will take me in. They can hide me or even get me further north so I can get away and start a new life in peace."

"You know these friends can pull that off?"

"Oh, yes. They used to be a part of the Underground

Railroad during the war, and they still know ways to get north that nobody else does. They're ready to help, so all I have to do is get there." Although there were no more tears to be seen, she looked down as fear crept into the corners of her eyes. "Them killers never got as close as they did tonight. I still don't know how I survived. I . . . I know I won't make it much longer without someone to protect me."

Clint thought about what the woman had said. Not all of it made complete sense, but his own eyes told him that she wasn't lying about everything. As for the rest of her tale, he was just interested enough that he wanted to see how it turned out.

Besides, he knew he needed to put Labyrinth behind him for a little while. All he'd been waiting for was a way to decide which direction he should take when he left town. North was as good as any other. And it had been a while since he'd last seen Oklahoma.

Clint smiled and pat Emma's hand. "I've had a lot of people ask for my help before. But I don't think I've ever had anyone do it in such a roundabout way."

She took the comment exactly as it was intended and laughed a little, despite everything else that she was feeling. "I just thought you should know what you'd be getting yourself into is all. After what happened to Darryl, I don't want to be responsible for anyone else getting hurt on my account."

"Did you pull the trigger on the gun that killed Darryl?" Clint asked.

"No."

"And did you hire the men that killed him?"

"Of course not."

"Then you're not responsible for his death. All that kind of thinking is going to get you is heartache that'll be with you for the rest of your life. Whatever you've been told about this curse, just put it aside. If it doesn't exist, then you'll just be wasting your life worrying about a mean-spirited ghost story."

"And what if it does exist?" Emma asked.

"In that case, there's not a lot you can do about it. Either way, you're better off just trying to get some rest. You've had a long night and we've got a long road ahead of us."

"So you'll take me?"

"I'll take you."

Clint gave Emma the key to his room at the Lone Star Hotel. "This will get you into my room. You can rest there while I clear up a few things."

"Is it safe?"

"Nobody's got more people after their hides than me and I've never had any trouble getting to sleep in that room. Besides, I'll be watching out for you."

For the first time since they'd met, Emma looked as though she was truly at ease. Her shoulders were no longer tensed, and even the pattern of her breathing slowed down as the thumping of her heart quieted to a more normal beat. All of this was reflected in the way she allowed herself to close her eyes and keep them closed.

Watching her, Clint swore he could see the fear bleeding out of her like rainwater falling away from a branch drying in the newly risen sun. But there was something else he felt at that moment. It was something much more familiar, even though it was far from a pleasant sensation.

"Come on," he said as he got up from the table and scanned the room carefully. "I'll take you to the Lone Star and make sure you get in the room safely."

Emma got to her feet easily, but when she saw the expression on Clint's face, she grabbed his hand and held it tightly. "Is something wrong?"

"I don't know yet," Clint replied. "I just got a feeling that something's not right."

Glancing around the room, Clint saw the same men at

the same tables they'd been at for the entire night. He looked toward the front door and found a few figures standing near the bar or next to the entrance. There were some shapes moving in the shadows outside as well, but nothing that should have put him on the defensive.

Knowing better than to ignore the feeling completely, Clint slipped his arm around Emma's shoulder so he could guide her without making it look like he thought anything was wrong.

"Just to be safe," he whispered, "let's head out the back door."

Emma nodded and followed Clint's lead. As she made her way around the tables and other gamblers, she could feel a familiar feeling of dread settle in the pit of her stomach. She knew that feeling only too well.

She'd felt it the last time she'd seen her father alive.

And she'd felt it while listening to Darryl breathing in the dark beside her.

TWENTY-FIVE

Grayfeather held the gun to Rhyne's head, watching the way the gunman's features twitched and twisted with every second that passed. He knew if he stood there long enough, the other man would tell him everything he needed to know without Grayfeather having to utter a single word. But the Sioux didn't have enough time for that. Instead, he would have to get what information he could using much cruder methods.

"I'm trying to warn you," Rhyne said in a voice that would have been solid enough to convince almost anybody of his good intentions.

Grayfeather wrapped his other hand around the back of Rhyne's head and pushed the gun barrel even harder against his skull. The Indian's strength brought a painful grimace to Rhyne's face as a bruise began to blacken the skin beneath the pistol's steel.

"Enough of that," Grayfeather said. "I want you to answer my question. After all the time you've been with me on this hunt, why have you chosen this moment to turn against me?"

The lies swam behind Rhyne's face like sharks circling beneath the surface of the ocean. For a couple of seconds, he fought to decide which of the sharks he should call to the top and which of the lines he'd prepared in advance he should try out on the Indian looming before him.

But as Grayfeather stared at him, patiently waiting for an excuse to pull his trigger, Rhyne knew that none of the lies would be enough to get him out of this room alive. He knew, without knowing how he knew, that the other man could tell truth from a lie with nothing more than a properly aimed glance.

"You want to know why?" Rhyne said, without truly expecting a response. "It's because of this job. Killing ain't no problem. Hell, even killing a woman ain't no problem for me. But we've been chasing down this one for some time now and when we get a chance to put an end to it, you let her get away."

"You don't need to know about my hunt," Grayfeather rasped. "You only need to do what you're told."

At that moment, through the open door, the sound of hushed voices could be heard coming from the end of the hall. After a whispered exchange, the shuffle of feet upon the stairs filtered into Rhyne's ears, bringing a relieved smile to his face.

"Yeah, well, that's the part I have a problem with," Rhyne said. "You see . . . I don't work for you no more. In fact, I'm about to get the rest of my money another way." Using all the strength he could get out of the muscles in his neck, Rhyne managed to pull himself away from Grayfeather's pistol and turn his head toward the open door. "Somebody help me!" he shouted. "This killer's got a gun on me!"

No surprise showed up on Grayfeather's face. Not even the slightest hint of shock over what had happened was evident on his hard, cold features. Rather than allow himself to get angry about what the other man had just done, he simply stared into Rhyne's face and said, "Her dark-

ness has touched your life just as it has corrupted mine.
You know that, don't you?"

"All I know is that you're on your own, red man. And
if you kill me, they'll just hang you that much faster."

"Is that why you did this?" Grayfeather asked as a dis-
believing smile appeared on his lips. "To protect yourself
from me?"

"I ain't afraid of you. But a man's got to cover his
tracks all the same. Workin' with Injuns for so long taught
me that."

The footsteps reached the top of the stairs, followed by
several sets of voices issuing quick commands back and
forth to one another. Grayfeather ignored them all, keeping all of his attention focused on the man who was still
squirming to break completely free from his grasp.

"You are afraid of me," the Sioux pointed out. "But
the person you should have feared is the same one you're
allowing to leave this place. When that woman goes to
another town and infects it with her curse, the deaths that
follow will be on *your* head." He lowered his gun and
slid it back into its holster. But before Rhyne could pull
away from him, Grayfeather clapped his hand back onto
the gunman's forehead, holding it steady in a viselike
grip.

"Let go of me, red man," Rhyne said, suddenly unable
to keep the fear from leaking into his words. "Those men
coming for you are the law. You hurt me and they'll shoot
you dow—"

"If you pray to any god, you should make your peace
with him. And when you lie in your bed in all the nights
that follow this one, think back to this moment as the one
when you yourself have doomed your soul."

TWENTY-SIX

Suddenly, the entire hallway was filled with noise similar to the arrival of a steam engine. Boots pounded against the floor, sending ripples beneath the feet of everyone on that floor. Voices shouted out at once in a chaotic mush, until finally one voice differentiated itself from the rest.

"You there!" the sheriff cried out as he charged to the front of his men and the open door of Grayfeather's room. "Let that man go and put your hands in the air."

The same deputy that Rhyne had spoken to was standing in the open doorway next to the town's head lawman. Pointing to Rhyne, he hollered, "What the hell are you doing here?"

Rhyne tried to look toward the peace officers, but was unable to turn his head. "I wanted to make sure he was still here, Sheriff. He said he was gonna kill me as soon as you boys ran up the stairs."

Grayfeather's voice was a calm whisper that somehow rumbled like thunder through Rhyne's head. "After a lifetime of lying, it's amazing you're not better at it than this."

And before the gunman could spit back his reply, Rhyne felt himself being dragged across the floor to the

110

doorway, and turned to face the line of lawmen that had
formed in the hallway leading to Grayfeather's room, the
sheriff and the deputy backing away from the room to
join the other lawmen. The Sioux still had a hold of the
back of Rhyne's head, gripping hard enough to cause
Rhyne's ears to ring as dim clouds formed in his vision.

Without saying another word, Grayfeather stepped behind Rhyne, using the gunman as a shield. Unlike the
other men in the immediate vicinity, the Indian's feet
barely made a sound as they moved away over the boards
toward the end of the hall.

"Stop right there," the sheriff yelled. "There ain't nowhere for you to go. If you come along with us quietly,
we'll see you get a legal trial and a chance to defend
yourself."

Grayfeather listened to the sheriff's words, even though
he had no intention of heeding them. He simply backed
away down the hall, walking steadily closer to where it
ended in a large window covered with dark red curtains.
He held Rhyne up high enough to block any bullets that
might be sent in his direction. The gunman wasn't big
enough to protect him completely, but Rhyne's body was
enough to shield the vital areas.

The sheriff followed the retreating pair slowly, making
sure not to do anything too suddenly in case the big Indian
was holding a gun or knife to the other man's back. His
deputies stayed right next to him, all of them young and
eager to bring down their target.

Stepping backward down the hall, Grayfeather didn't
stop until the back of his heel touched the wall at the end
of the hall. Focusing on the skin of his back and shoulders, he pressed himself against the solid surface to get a
rough feel for the size and structure of the window there.

The sheriff was shouting something else at him, but he
didn't waste the energy required to listen. Instead, Grayfeather pulled Rhyne a little closer and whispered fiercely

into his ear, "Remember what I told you. And remember how you let that woman get away. You'll see her again. But when you do, it will be through a dead man's eyes."

And with that, the Sioux leaned forward and snapped himself back, breaking the glass with the impact of his body against the window, letting go of Rhyne half a second before taking the gunman outside with him.

Grayfeather closed his eyes and pictured the view from the window as he'd seen it the first time he'd examined it after arriving at the hotel. He blocked out the pain coming from the bruised bones in his back as well as the glass lodged in his flesh. Pushing off of the windowsill with the tips of his boots, he used that last bit of motion to toss himself into empty air, confident that he would be able to sail just past the ground floor's awning.

The front of his body scraped along the edge of the awning, and Grayfeather turned his head the instant before he caught a wooden shingle beneath the chin. Timber snapped and groaned as he caught the awning beneath his fingertips. Although the flimsy structure didn't hold, the awning was enough to slow Grayfeather's fall before he crashed to the ground.

Taking a moment to get his bearings, Grayfeather checked himself over to make sure that he hadn't sustained any serious injuries besides the ones he already knew about. Other than the glass and bruising, the only parts of him that hurt were his legs and feet from absorbing the fall. He shoved that pain aside as well, and ducked around the building to disappear in the alley just as the sheriff and his men stuck their heads out of the broken window.

Voices echoed through the air and gunshots crackled behind him as Grayfeather dashed away from the hotel. He could tell that the shots weren't getting anywhere near him, but he kept running nonetheless. As he made his way toward the livery where his horse was waiting, the Sioux broke out of the other side of the alley and slowed to a quick walk.

He could only imagine how he looked. The hot flow of blood coursed down his back, and his joints sent steady jolts of pain with every step he took. And even though he knew the sheriff would be after him, Grayfeather didn't think about leaving Labyrinth.

He couldn't get himself to do such a thing when there was still so much left to be done there.

The very thought of abandoning his mission at this point was akin to thinking of a way to change the color of his flesh. Such a thing was just impossible, so there was no reason to waste precious energy even thinking about it.

What he was doing was too important to abandon now. No matter how many partners stabbed him in the back or how many lawmen were out for his blood. The only thing that mattered was the fact that Emma Deerborne was still out there and her curse was gaining power with every breath she took.

Stopping for a second to slow his breath, Grayfeather allowed himself to rest for a few seconds while he thought about his next move. He knew that Emma had come here looking for help, which also meant that he knew where she could be found.

With that thought in mind, the Sioux clenched his teeth against the sharp pains shooting through his body and headed out in search of the man named Clint Adams.

The hunt continued.

TWENTY-SEVEN

Riding out of Labyrinth wasn't as hard as Clint thought it would be. In fact, Clint felt more than a little relieved after saddling up Eclipse and stocking up on supplies that he would need while on the trail. The night before should have gone by painfully slowly, especially considering that he couldn't even spend it in the comfort of his own bed.

The moment Emma had lain down upon the comfortable mattress, her eyes shut, and they didn't open again until the sun was in the sky. More than that, when Clint came back to wake her up, he was fairly certain that she hadn't even moved from the position she was in when he'd last left her.

As for himself, he'd figured on spending the night in another room in the Lone Star Hotel, but had never actually gotten around to picking up a key. Instead, he'd spent his last few hours in town making his rounds and saying his good-byes to all the friends he would be leaving behind. Besides Rick Hartman, there was also the owner of the Lone Star, Lily McGearson. The voluptuous brunette had spent many a night with him both in his bed and out on the town. Hers was a face he was certainly going to miss, which was why he made his farewell short and sweet. No more than a drink shared with her and Hartman at Rick's Place.

Clint had never been big on drawn-out good-byes. The closer it came to dawn, the more convinced he became that it was time for him to go. The trail was calling for him, and it would certainly be good to get back to the wandering he'd known for the better part of his life.

"You can settle when you're dead," Hartman had said for his final toast. "We'll be here when you pass through West Texas again."

And that was all that needed to be said. In fact, both Hartman and Lily acted as though they'd been expecting Clint to leave a lot earlier than this. Deep down inside, Clint was thinking the same thing.

Now, with the sun cresting over the horizon in a way that painted the sky in lush reds and vibrant yellows, Clint packed his belongings and secured the saddlebags onto Eclipse's back. The Darley Arabian stallion fidgeted from one foot to another, anxious to get moving and raring to stretch his legs for more than the hour or two he'd been granted while he'd been put up at the town's livery.

Emma's horse had been at the same livery as well, which saved Clint the trouble of going to fetch the animal after breakfast. Once she climbed into her saddle, she seemed every bit as anxious to leave as Eclipse.

"How long will it take us to get to Oklahoma?" she asked once Clint was done with his last-minute preparations.

Clint swung his leg over Eclipse's back and settled into the familiar groove of his saddle. "Shouldn't be more than a few days." Eclipse jostled beneath him, already trotting toward the front door. "Then again, by the way Eclipse is acting, we might just get there by tomorrow afternoon. I've got a feeling that Eclipse will want to run the whole way."

"I know how he feels," Emma replied, keeping right beside him.

"Then let's not waste all this energy." And with that, Clint let the Darley Arabian trot outside before pointing him in the right direction and snapping the reins.

That was all Eclipse needed before breaking into a gallop and thundering toward Labyrinth's outskirts. Emma's ride wasn't able to keep up completely, but she managed to keep fairly close until they got into the open range. Once there was nothing around them besides clean, empty air and a long stretch of trail, both horses lowered their heads and taxed their muscles to the limit.

TWENTY-EIGHT

Feeling the wind in his face and watching the land speed past him in a continuous blur of motion, Clint realized just how much he'd missed this feeling of complete freedom. He couldn't have wiped the grin off his face if he'd tried. When he looked back to check on Emma, he saw that she wasn't having much difficulty at all keeping up the pace.

With her hair flowing in the rushing wind and her body moving fluidly on top of her horse, Emma looked like a completely different person than the one that had found Clint the previous night. The difference was more than what could be accomplished by a change of clothes or even a solid night's sleep. She had a strength now that seemed to flow from every one of her pores, bathing her with a glow that made her seem so much more radiant than before. Even more . . . alive.

That was it.

Turning back to look at the trail ahead, Clint knew that he'd put his finger on the change inside her exactly. She seemed more alive than the previous night. There was no more of the fearful, fidgeting little thing that had been almost ready to hide beneath the table at the Lucky

117

Queen. In her place, there was a strong woman, confident in her actions and ready to take charge of her life.

Clint could see that in her eyes as well as in the sureness of her movements. Without consciously meaning to, he found himself turning around every couple of seconds to get another look at her. And every time he did, he found her looking right back at him, holding his eyes with her own and smiling warmly by way of thanking him for the new day he'd given her.

He wasn't sure how long they rode like that, flat out and charging into the wind, but when Eclipse's breaths started getting heavier, Clint pulled back on the reins and brought the stallion down to a more easygoing pace.

Emma pulled up alongside him, her expression looking more like she was out on a casual day's ride instead of fleeing from a town where someone had tried to kill her the night before. "That's quite an animal," she said while looking at Eclipse.

"You're right about that. Sometimes it's all I can do to keep from being thrown off of him when he gets too anxious."

"Why do I think it'd be next to impossible for you to get thrown off that horse?"

"I guess we do know each other pretty well. So where is this medicine man we're after? I'll need a little more information to know which way to ride."

"He's on a small reservation near the Arkansas border. Part of the Caddo tribe."

Figuring the distance in his head, Clint squinted and ran through his mental calculations. "That might take a little more time than I thought, but we should still make it within a week."

"If you're worried about the Apaches around here, don't think anything of it," Emma said. "I've got some friends in the area and their names should go a long ways in getting us through where most travelers aren't usually too welcome."

"I don't have too many problems with most of the tribes. Usually, we tend to leave each other alone, but if you can get us through some of the trickier spots, then that should shave some time off our trip."

For the next few moments, the only sound either of them could hear was the steady rhythm of the horses' hooves against the ground and the animals' breathing as they recovered from their run. It was a perfect day for travel. The sun was hot on their backs, but the wind was strong enough to cool them off. An occasional bank of clouds rolled over their heads to give them a break from the constant summer glare.

Clint and Emma whiled away the next several hours talking about their lives and getting better acquainted with one another. Despite the conflicting signals he'd gotten when they'd first met, Clint couldn't help but grow to like Emma over the course of the day.

Her voice was soft and melodic, making even the most mundane things a pleasure to listen to. Her skin picked up a colorful hue as more time passed under the sun and she only seemed to become more comfortable with the open spaces around her and the wind tussling her hair.

They eventually saw a small town in the distance that wasn't more than a cluster of shacks half a mile off the beaten path. As much as Clint wanted to keep going, he knew it wouldn't do anyone any good to wear themselves out on the first day. Just as he was about to suggest stopping at the town to Emma, something caught his attention out of the corner of his eye.

With a tug on the reins, he brought Eclipse to a stop.

"What's the matter?" Emma asked when she noticed the stern, intense look on Clint's face.

For a few seconds, Clint didn't reply. When he saw that Emma was going to ask her question again, he lifted his hand and stopped her words before they had a chance to leave her mouth.

Although Clint hadn't seen exactly what it was that made him feel so uneasy, he knew there had been something. Whatever it was had almost been out of his field of vision, but was just enough to send a warning chill through his bones, causing his instincts to take over from there.

Clint was just about to write off his feeling to nerves when he saw it again.

There . . . on the horizon just south of their position was a subtle hint of movement. Anywhere else and that same movement might have gone unnoticed. But since Clint was already on the lookout for anything unusual or anyone trailing after him and Emma, that single movement was enough to put him on the defensive.

As if he was getting confirmation of his suspicion, Clint saw the faint glimmer of sunlight bouncing off a reflective surface. The light winked at him, and was gone in the next instant. Its job was done, however, and Clint knew that he wasn't just imagining things.

"Clint, what's the matter?" Emma asked in a hushed, urgent tone.

"We're being followed."

TWENTY-NINE

Emma drew in a sharp breath and brought her hand up to her mouth, as if to catch it before she made too much noise. Her eyes turned into wide, green orbs as she looked nervously between Clint and the spot he was studying on the horizon.

"I knew I shouldn't have brought anyone else into this," she whispered. "I felt that something was wrong last night, but I put it aside and thought everything would be better if I could just get someone to help me get away."

Without taking his eyes away from what he'd seen, Clint reached into his saddlebag for the spyglass stored there. "What do you mean you felt something was wrong?" he asked while extending the telescope and putting it to his eye.

"That's the way the curse works. It lets me know something bad's going to happen just so I can be certain it was my fault when it finally comes. I shouldn't have brought you into this, Clint. There's nothing you can do for me now."

"You can stop that talk right now," he said while searching the surrounding land. "I'm not the type who gets forced into anything. I'm helping you because I decided to do so." Scanning the area once again, he couldn't find a single thing to point him in the right direction. Every branch on every tree seemed to be in place. The only things that moved were the leaves being pushed about by the wind.

Collapsing the spyglass with a flick of his wrist, Clint dropped it into the bag on Eclipse's flank and swung down from the saddle. "There's not a lot of places to hide out there," he said. "Maybe all I saw was an animal or something. Even if it is another rider, that doesn't mean they're even after us or want to do us any—"

The tall grass directly in front of Clint exploded with a flurry of motion similar to a flock of wild birds erupting from cover. No sooner had Clint heard it than he felt a dull pain in his stomach and the world tilting crazily around him.

Emma's screams filled his ears as Clint was taken off his feet to land heavily on his back. The instant he realized that someone's shoulder was driving the air from his lungs, the pressure was gone. Whoever had knocked him down was now rolling off to the side, disappearing almost instantly in a patch of tall grass.

Clint reacted without thinking, his legs coiling beneath him before springing out and pushing him away from the attacking figure. Although he landed awkwardly on his side, Clint was able to roll another few feet until he could plant his boots in the soil and stop his momentum with an outstretched hand.

Moving instinctively for his gun, Clint searched for a target in the knee-high grass. The first thing he saw was Emma hopping back to get away from the spot where Clint had been taken down. But then, just as Clint's hand found the Colt at his side, his eyes locked onto a figure crouching to his left, barreling forward with one hand extended and the other cocked back behind his head.

Clint didn't get a chance to look at the other man's

face. He was too busy throwing himself to one side as the figure's other hand lunged forward. Pushing off with both feet, Clint didn't have to see whatever it was the attacker was holding to know that it was dangerous and coming straight toward him.

Something whistled through the air, lashing toward Clint's face in a deadly arc that stopped just short of digging into the bridge of his nose. Clint felt as though everything slowed down around him as something resembling a crude hatchet passed in front of his eyes, moving so quickly that he was surprised to catch even the faintest glance of it at all.

Once the other man's arm reached its limit and the hatchet swung back toward its owner, Clint turned away from his attacker just long enough to look at where he was going to land. In the rush to get out of harm's way, his only worry had been to move. Now, Clint had to make sure he landed at least somewhat gracefully. Otherwise, the next time he saw that hatchet, it would be buried deep in his flesh.

Twisting at his waist and bending in ways that sent pain tearing through his body, Clint managed to end his roll with his feet beneath him. The moment his boots touched the ground, Clint was staggering to his feet. In another flicker of motion, his hand snapped down and was gripping the Colt when it came back up.

His eyes darted to the last spot where he'd seen the figure that had tackled him, finding nothing but empty space and waving grass.

There was another rustle of the hairs at the back of Clint's neck, which was more than enough to get him moving. Remembering the first attack, Clint ducked down low and tensed his muscles less than half a second before the darting figure came at him a third time.

This time, Clint had prepared himself enough to avoid the hatchet, which sliced through the air above his head.

He clenched his jaw and looked at the man swinging the weapon, getting a quick look at Grayfeather's face before the Sioux brought an elbow crashing down on the spot where Clint's shoulder met his neck.

Clint had been expecting another fist or even a boot to be following close after the hatchet, which was why he'd tensed beforehand. Although the Indian's elbow wasn't completely expected, the blow landed on solid muscle, causing a dull pain that was easily washed away by the urgency racing through Clint's veins.

Even though he was able to shrug away the pain, Clint still felt his knees start to give way and his legs buckle from the force of the impact. He knew well enough that the Indian had hit a nerve, which meant that the other man was more than just quick on his feet and quiet as a mouse. He was also a trained fighter.

That was never a good thing to learn in the middle of a scuffle.

Clint twisted at the waist while bringing up his left arm to hook around the Indian's shoulder. With one fluid motion, he bent forward and down, bringing the Indian into the air and off his feet. Although Clint was hoping to gain some sort of advantage with that maneuver, all he got was an extra second or two.

THIRTY

The Indian twisted like a cat through the air, somehow turning himself upright so he could land on his feet. This time, it was Grayfeather who took a moment to stop and study his opponent. The Indian crouched down until he was almost on his hands and knees, tossing his tomahawk from one hand to another while his eyes took in his opponent.

He'd heard of Clint Adams in stories passed through saloons as well as in the newspapers. In all that time, however, he'd assumed that Adams couldn't possibly be the indestructible legend that some people said he was. Although far from indestructible, the man in front of the Sioux was indeed formidable.

That, however, wouldn't change The Gunsmith's fate.

Grayfeather could kill him. Deep down inside, he was certain of that.

Watching the other man's stance, Grayfeather decided that he would only be slitting his own throat if he cut Adams short. So rather than play with him any longer, he decided to end the battle as quickly as he could before moving on the woman. Besides, he figured enough of the woman's curse had soaked into Adams's spirit to

125

damn The Gunsmith to a quick death. It was only a matter of time.

Having made a point to strike before any weapons were drawn, Grayfeather figured that Adams would be like most other gunfighters who were useless without their pistols in hand. The Sioux was about to throw himself forward to strike the fatal blow when he noticed that Adams had somehow gotten his hands on his gun.

Grayfeather hadn't seen the other man clear leather. In fact, he hadn't even seen him make a move in that direction. It was as though the spirits themselves had armed The Gunsmith for this fight.

Fine, Grayfeather thought. If that's the way it's to be, then that's how it would be.

All of these thoughts took no more than a second or two to pass through the Sioux's mind. Shifting his weight between one foot and the other, he faked the motion of tossing his tomahawk back into his right hand before surging forward like a charging ram.

A gunshot thundered over Grayfeather's head as he lunged. The bite of lead into his flesh sent pain spiking through his left side, but that wasn't enough to divert his intentions. Grayfeather centered his attack on Clint's midsection in an attempt to gut the gunfighter, but another stronger wave of pain caused him to stumble slightly when he took his next step.

It wasn't much more than a minor falter, but it caused the Sioux to pause for half a second to regain his footing. When he set himself back into his attack, the gunfighter was no longer in the same place as before. In fact, Adams was twisting just fast enough to avoid the incoming tomahawk before its stone blade could slice him open.

Clint studied the Indian as both men took a second to get a good look at their opponent. Like two predators, they sized each other up before committing to their next attack.

Knowing he wouldn't have enough time to try to talk to the Indian, Clint decided to take the other man down the instant he tried attacking him again.

Keeping his eyes on what he now knew to be a tomahawk, Clint watched as the Indian tossed it from hand to hand while shifting on his feet. Such movements were classic tactics used by knife fighters to distract their opponents as well as throw them off guard. Clint knew this well enough that he didn't buy the other man's fake toss, which would come before the next strike.

Sure enough, the Indian moved as though he were switching hands again right before lunging toward Clint. But the other man moved so fast that Clint wasn't certain if the switch was a fake or not. Running on instinct, he took a shot at the incoming figure and twisted out of the way, assuming the tomahawk was being held right-handed.

Even as he spun on the balls of his feet, Clint could still see the spray of blood that had come from the Indian's left side. Since the other man had been crouched down low, the bullet had torn through him like a tiger's claws, leaving a deep, bloody groove lengthwise over his body.

Clint could feel the other man pass by him. The tomahawk once again whistled through the air, but the blade came nowhere near him. Thanking his lucky stars that he'd been right about the Indian's maneuver, Clint continued his motion and swung the back of his left hand in a tight sweeping motion that landed heavily on the other man's ribs.

THIRTY-ONE

When Clint felt his backhand connect, he hoped that might be enough to keep the Indian from taking another shot right away. Having developed an eye for speed and a knack for summing up the threat any given man posed, Clint knew he had to tackle this Indian one move at a time.

Thinking ahead any further than that might have slowed him down just a fraction of a second. And in that amount of time, an opponent like this could snuff out anyone's life like a candle.

Clint sensed the Indian's body pass around behind him. Counting on the fact that the tomahawk would probably be sailing toward him at any moment, he whipped around as fast as he could with the Colt ready to fire.

Something brushed by his wrist before he could complete his turn, so Clint pointed the gun in that direction and fired. By the time he blinked his eyes, he was facing the direction where the brush had come from, half of his muscles already tensing for the next offensive or defensive move.

With the gunshot echoing over the trail and within his ears, Clint couldn't hear another thing besides his heart slamming against the inside of his ribs. The grass listed back and forth, but other than that there was no other movement he could see.

Clint took a quick look over his shoulder, hoping that the Indian hadn't already gotten to Emma. But the woman was still near the horses, scared and hunkering down low, but otherwise exactly where he'd left her.

"Are you all right?" Clint asked.

Emma looked up as though she was afraid to take her hands away from her face. "Y-yes . . ." she said meekly. That was when she spotted the blood on Clint's collar. "Oh, my God. You're hurt!"

At first, Clint didn't know what she was talking about. Then his hand went up to investigate a nagging twinge on his neck. The skin there felt warm and damp. When he pulled it away, he saw that his fingertips were covered in blood.

The sight surprised him more than anything else, and when he touched that spot again, he felt where his skin had been broken. "It's nothing," he told her while looking carefully all around. "Just a scratch."

Emma dashed over to him and started dabbing at the wound with a scarf that had been tied around her neck. Clint accepted her care as he searched for any trace of where the Indian had gone. There weren't a lot of places to go besides a few trees and the tall grass. Even so, there would have been something to give away the other man's position. A patch of flattened weeds. A shadow. Anything.

But there was nothing.

Clint walked toward the edge of a thicker patch of grass, watching for the Indian to give himself away. But even as he did so, he knew he wasn't going to see anything. Relating to the other man as one predator to another, Clint knew on a basic level that the confrontation was over. At least for now anyway.

He heard something coming closer to him, but he didn't

bother to look. Clint knew it was only Emma making her way to stand by his side.

"Let me see to that for you," she said while reaching out to tend to the scratch at his neck. "It may not be that deep, but it still needs to be looked after before it gets any worse."

Her hands felt good as they gently wiped away the blood that had crusted on his skin. Every once in a while she would hit on a tender spot that would send a small twinge beneath Clint's skin, but it was barely enough to attract his attention.

What troubled Clint more was the fact that he didn't remember getting that wound in the first place. As many times as he ran over the fight in his mind, he couldn't recall that tomahawk getting so close to slicing open his throat. With one lightning-fast move flowing into the next, the whole thing must've only lasted a few seconds. And if the Indian's cut had been an inch or so deeper, Clint could very well be bleeding out at this very moment.

"Are you sure you're all right?" Emma asked as she finished up with Clint's scratch.

Clint nodded, and allowed himself to stop looking for the Indian and turn his eyes toward her. "You need to tell me everything you know about that man."

"But I already—"

"No, Emma! All you said was that he's been chasing after you. But there's got to be more than that. I've never seen someone fight that way."

She turned her eyes away and lowered her head. "His name is John Grayfeather. He's been learning to fight since he could walk. He could've killed me so many times. Even after Darryl got shot . . . he let me go. I don't know why, but he let me go."

Suddenly, her eyes grew wide and she looked quickly around her. "Is he going to come back?"

"No," Clint replied. "If he still wanted to fight, he wouldn't have left."

"Are you sure? How could you know for sure?"

Clint listened to the primal instinct that ruled a man in times of life-and-death situations. The part of him that was a fighter, the lethal part dwelling deep inside, told him the danger had passed. "Trust me," he said. "He's gone, but he'll be back. I think I put up a better fight than he was used to."

At that moment, Clint's hand drifted up to the scratch on his neck. If he'd leaned in the wrong direction just once . . .

"What do we do now?" Emma asked.

"We move on. Either that, or we can sit right here and wait for him to sneak up on us again."

"But what about next time?"

That was the question that sat in the back of Clint's mind ever since he'd started living by the gun. It didn't matter that he only used the Colt to defend himself or others. What mattered was that he needed that gun to stay alive. It was a tool essential for survival in a world filled with men who would just as soon kill him as ask for the time.

Those men would never stop.

There would always be a next time.

Clint walked up to Emma and put his hands on her shoulders. He could feel the trembling in her body, which instantly subsided beneath his touch. He moved his hands down to her waist, which was all Emma needed to press herself against him and hold him close.

"You can't worry about what might happen," he said. "Just go on with what you need to do. If you curl up and hide for the rest of your days, then your life is just as over as if Grayfeather had shot you down. The only way to beat him is to keep living. That's how you beat them all."

Emma's body seemed to melt into Clint's. Her arms cinched around him as though she was hanging onto him for dear life and would never let go. Looking up at him, she smiled warmly, slipped a hand behind his head, and pulled him down a bit so she could kiss him gently on the lips.

"That's got to be the best advice I've ever gotten," she said softly.

Smiling, Clint said, "Well, you'd better enjoy it then. Because I'm not exactly known for my good advice. In fact, I seem to bring trouble with me wherever I go."

Emma couldn't help but laugh. The melodic sound surrounded them both, and even lingered in Clint's ears while she kissed him deeply on the mouth. This time, her lips parted and her tongue slipped into Clint's mouth, allowing her to taste him as their hearts pounded wildly against each other.

As much as Clint hated to do it, he broke off from her embrace and led Emma to her horse. "I said that Indian was done for now. That doesn't mean he won't come back if he sees we're too preoccupied."

After climbing into her saddle, Emma said, "Then we'll just have to get preoccupied some other time."

THIRTY-TWO

The sheriff in Labyrinth didn't know squat.

Douglas Rhyne knew that much before talking to him, but he'd hoped that he could at least get a partial bounty out of him for identifying Grayfeather. But no matter how much he tried to persuade the lawman, he wasn't able to get a dime for himself.

Of course, he didn't have any trouble getting out of the charge of killing that man who'd been traveling with Emma Deerborne. There'd been a few people who'd seen Rhyne and the Indian leave the hotel, but they were too scared to say much of anything while Rhyne was right there looking at them.

Although he knew he wouldn't be able to come back to Labyrinth anytime soon, he had no reason to go back to that place anyway. Just to be safe, he cleared out of there as soon as he left the sheriff's office. When he hit the trail, he had plenty of time to think about all that had happened in the last couple of days.

He'd gotten a fair amount of cash out of the red man, but that source of income was now officially dried up. He'd been thinking that the sheriff and an entire bunch of his men would have been enough to take down Grayfeather and put a fat reward in his own pocket, but that idea had blown up as well.

All that was left was for Rhyne to go back to living off his own wits, which was what he'd been doing for the better part of his life. The gunman headed out of town, thinking about the last thing Grayfeather had said just before leaping out of that window like some kind of damned bird.

Maybe it was all the time he had to himself during the slow ride out of town. It could have even been the sun beating down on his head for too long, but Rhyne was actually starting to think that some of what the Injun had said wasn't a bunch of crap after all.

Perhaps there was something to that bitch's curse.

He had seen just about every one of the woman's men get killed one way or another. And even though he'd been the one to kill a few of them, that didn't change the fact that they'd all wound up dead. All the way back to her own daddy, the men in her life had turned up dead. That was why Grayfeather was getting paid so much to get rid of her.

Rhyne shook his head as he leaned back a bit in the saddle. If only he'd been the one the folks back in Dakota had hired for the job, he would be the one sitting on top of all that money. Hell, if it had been up to him, that woman would have been dead a long time ago.

Suddenly, Rhyne's head snapped up and his eyes went wide. At that moment, he barely even noticed the movements of the horse beneath him or the scenery all around. He even forgot about the law back in Labyrinth that would be coming after him as soon as a couple of witnesses found their nerve again.

The only thing rattling through Rhyne's skull was the money that Grayfeather always seemed to have at any given moment. He knew the Indian had been given some cash for expenses, and that Grayfeather even got more money from local tribes that knew about what he was doing.

After what had happened in Labyrinth and how they'd parted ways, the last thing the red man would expect was to see Rhyne's face again. He had his hands full with Clint Adams right now, and although the Injun was too stupid to take someone like Adams seriously, Rhyne knew better than that.

Rhyne knew about The Gunsmith and just how good that man was supposed to be. Even if he was half as good as the stories going around about him, he should be more than enough to keep Grayfeather on his toes. Adams might just be the one to bury that no-good Injun no matter how many fancy tricks Grayfeather had up his sleeve.

All Adams would need was a little help from someone who knew a thing or two about Grayfeather's style. Maybe a few pointers on the Injun's weaknesses. And once Grayfeather was dead, Rhyne could sweep in and relieve him of all that money he carried.

But more than that, he could put a bullet through that little woman's brain and drag her carcass back to Dakota so he could claim the big reward for himself. With the rest of those Indians so worried about their curse, they would be happy just to have that bitch dead. They would pay and accept any story Rhyne gave them about where Grayfeather ran off to.

Rhyne's face lit up with a beaming smile. He knew where the woman was headed, since he'd been with Grayfeather the day they got that information from another one of her dearly departed guides. All he had to do was catch up to her.

Turning his horse toward the east, Rhyne touched his heels to the animal's sides and snapped the reins. His mare broke into a run, and would keep running until Rhyne could track down Adams and the woman. After that, all he'd have to do was rake in the money.

"Curse, my ass." Rhyne laughed to himself. "I'm gonna be the curse on all three of their hides."

THIRTY-THREE

Compared to their meeting with Grayfeather, the rest of the day passed by so quietly that Clint and Emma barely noticed it had gone. Just as Clint's eyelids were starting to get heavy and his body was starting to feel the rigors of hours in the saddle, they came within sight of the small town Clint had been aiming for. It wasn't much on the eyes, but the town had a hotel and a place to eat, which was all they needed.

Within the hour, Clint and Emma rode into the small settlement of Barrow, Texas. They made a line straight for what they thought was a restaurant, only to find that the place had been boarded up for so long that the nails keeping the door shut were already rusty.

"This doesn't look good," Clint said as he pulled on the door's handle just to be sure.

But the door didn't budge, and there wasn't so much as a peep from inside the small building.

"How long has it been since you've been here?" Emma asked, her arms crossed over her chest.

Clint's first reaction was to say it hadn't been long at all. It seemed as though he'd been through here no more than a few months ago, but when he actually thought back to exact dates, those few months became more like a few years.

Once again, Clint felt the weight of the years pressing down on his shoulders. "It hasn't been that long," he said in his defense. "At least, not long enough for this whole town to go under."

Emma looked across the street, where she saw nothing but a few empty porches and several broken windows. Turning to glance down the road one way and then the other, she shook her head slowly at the rushing sound of wind whistling through rotten wood.

"Well, maybe everyone's at church," she said after turning back to face Clint.

"Sure. If that church is in a whole other town. I hate to say it, but this place feels dead."

But Emma wasn't about to give up so early. Rather than climb back onto her horse, she led the animal toward a taller building near the end of the street. Clint looked to see where she was going, and noticed the faded "HOTEL" sign nailed above the door of that bigger building.

When he got closer, Clint saw that the sign actually read "H EL."

Shaking his head, he reluctantly followed behind Emma. "That is most definitely not a good sign," he grumbled to himself.

The only things left of the hotel besides the sign and four walls, which were one strong breeze away from falling in on each other, were a few bed frames and four chairs. Emma wanted to investigate the upper level, but since the stairs almost collapsed under her first step, they both decided not to put any faith at all in the floors above them.

Two rooms were on the first floor. One had an empty bed frame, and the other contained two of the four chairs, plus a mattress that had been made into a comfortable home for a large family of mice. Once they left the hotel, neither one of them felt up to exploring any more of Barrow and they rode out of town.

"That," Clint said in frustration, "was one hell of a piece of bad luck. That was the only town around here that we could get to before sundown."

"So where does that leave us?"

"We can either ride awhile longer and make camp, or ride through the night until we get to the next town."

Emma cringed just a bit, started to say something, and then bit her lip. Finally, once the ruins of Barrow were behind them, she cringed again. "How long was it since you saw this next town?" she asked.

"I guess . . . no more than—"

"A few months?" Emma said.

Clint bit his own tongue and scowled over at Emma. Although the comment bit into his craw, he couldn't deny what she was pointing out to him. "Point taken," Clint said grudgingly. "But I don't know how comfortable I am making camp with Grayfeather on our tails. All he'd have to do is wait for us to sleep, sneak into camp, and pick us off. Hell, he's probably hoping we'd do something like that."

Shaking her head solemnly, Emma said, "Believe me, if he wants to get at us, locking ourselves in a hotel room won't slow him down much. I know that from personal experience."

Clint's mind was suddenly filled with grotesque images of the carnage he'd found in the room Emma had vacated back in Labyrinth. Although that didn't make him feel any better about camping out in the open, it did show that they would need something more than a lock on a door to keep them safe.

"I'll tell you what," Clint said after a few uncomfortable seconds had passed by in silence. "How about we head for that town and if we find it before we fall asleep in the saddle, we'll sleep there. If not, we'll find an open spot and sleep in shifts."

Emma's voice was surprisingly cheerful. She nodded crisply, regarding Clint with undisguised trust in her eyes. "That's about as good a plan as any. Besides, I know you'll keep me safe, Clint. You've been like a savior to me so far. I trust you."

They made the rest of the day's ride without saying too much to each other. While Clint kept his eyes and ears open for any sign that they were being followed or about to be ambushed, Emma seemed content to sit and quietly watch the sun fade away in the distance.

The sky darkened into a deep, purplish red, and then into a lush shade of orange. Finally, all the light faded away after one last, brilliant display, which splashed the sky full of breathtaking color. After that, the stars began appearing in clusters of glittering light, which eventually filled the black heavens like a great spill of diamonds.

"Guess we camp for the night," Clint said as he brought Eclipse to a stop in an open field of sparse grass bordered by thin, wispy saplings. "This is the best place to stop unless you wanted to push on any further tonight."

"No," Emma said while stretching her arms up over her head. "This is fine. I think I'm about to keel over anyway."

"Me too." Swinging down from the stallion's back, Clint stretched his back and started removing his supplies and bedroll from the back of his saddle. "I'll gather up some firewood and walk the perimeter. Could you gather up some rocks and clear away some of that grass?"

"I think I can handle that," Emma said sarcastically.

Clint tossed his saddlebags down. "There's some food in here. It's not much, but it should be enough to fill our stomachs."

Sensing Clint's distraction, Emma merely nodded in reply and went to the bags to see what she had to work with as far as dinner was concerned.

The campsite was perfect. Clint walked around the clearing and gathered up thick pieces of wood as well as an armload of thin, brittle branches. Keeping most of it for kindling, he spread out the rest of the thin branches around the edge of the camp, making sure to keep most of them hidden beneath leaves or what little grass there was.

In the dark, it would be difficult to see most of the branches, and impossible to see them all. They were just thin and dry enough to snap loudly if anything bigger than a groundhog stepped on them. It wouldn't be enough to make him feel completely safe, but it went a long way in the right direction.

Trying not to think about just how close Grayfeather actually was, Clint took the remaining wood to the middle of the camp and settled in for the night.

THIRTY-FOUR

The Sioux rode like a shadow that was able to break away from its source and return whenever it desired. After he'd slipped away from Adams, he got back to his horse and followed the gunfighter without being sensed more than any other uneasy feeling in the back of someone's mind.

He rode bareback on a brown and white gelding, so there wasn't even the sound of leather straps slapping against metal buckles to give away his position. Grayfeather kept himself far enough away from Adams that neither man could see the other. Every so often, the Sioux would cut ahead of Adams's path and wait for him to go by. Once he saw the distant figures, Grayfeather knew that he was still on the right path.

He rode like that all day long. Fading in and out. Conscious of every sound he made, from the leaves crunching underfoot to the wind that rustled in his wake.

The only time Grayfeather nearly broke his silence was when the day boiled away into night. Darkness was a mistress that normally worked to protect Grayfeather like a cloak passed down from the spirits themselves. This night, however, that mistress swallowed up Clint Adams along with the woman he was protecting, almost stealing both of them away from the Sioux's watchful eye.

Almost.

The moment Adams's shadow became indistinguishable from the rest, Grayfeather dismounted and led his horse with a hand over the animal's neck. Both man and beast knew to walk softly, which carried them forward slowly, but without making a sound.

After a few hours of traveling like that, Grayfeather found what he'd been looking for. He knew where the next town was, and was prepared to race there if he didn't catch up to Adams soon. But his patience was rewarded in the form of a thin wisp of smoke curling up into the sky. It would have been invisible if not for the fat, luminescent moon hanging in the sky like a pale-skinned guardian.

It could only have been the spirits that allowed that strand of smoke to drift over the face of the moon. And Grayfeather made sure to thank those spirits when he caught sight of the one thing that would lead him to the gunfighter's camp.

Taking a moment to whisper a prayer to the spirit of the hunt, Grayfeather left his horse behind and crept toward the source of the smoke on all fours. There wasn't much to use for cover, but he managed to press his body close to the ground and nestle himself beneath the sheltering arm of the mistress of darkness.

Every step was a carefully planned event.

Each movement was an exercise in strategic calculation, taking everything into account right down to the pebbles that might or might not be just beneath the thinnest layer of topsoil.

To those that didn't know any better, what Grayfeather did might have looked like magic. At the very least, it resembled something that should only be possible in legend. But Grayfeather was no legend. And he most certainly didn't proclaim to have any magic at his disposal.

Instead, the Sioux's silent motion and fighting skills were simply the result of a lifetime's worth of training at the hands of a few experts in the field. It was a Cherokee who had taught him to hunt and track. An old Tillamook had shared his secrets of moving silently and becoming one with the night. A drunken white man had showed Grayfeather the ways of the blade, and what he knew of a gun, Grayfeather had taught himself.

As for the way he moved when fighting in close combat, that had been passed on to him by a Chinaman who lived in the Nevada desert. There was no magic involved in any of it. Just a lot of watching and learning while the true masters revealed what they knew to someone who'd been willing to listen.

Grayfeather thought about that old Tillamook and the countless nights he'd followed the wise man through the forests in the northeast logging country. Although the Sioux wasn't half as stealthy as that old trickster, he'd learned enough to slip past most men without even raising a suspicion.

Indeed, most of the men that Grayfeather worked with thought he was a user of magic. That was the only way they could justify the Sioux's hard-earned skills.

Foolishness was all that was.

Grayfeather knew that there was no such thing as magic. The closest anyone came to magic was the medicine used by the tribal holy men. Even so, Grayfeather had a bad taste in his mouth from the few examples he'd seen of such medicine.

It was that kind of medicine that had unleashed the curse upon Emma Deerborne. And that, in turn, had taken the lives of more men than Grayfeather even cared to think about. That kind of medicine could only result in death. And it was too powerful for anyone to hope that it could be cured by anything but the most powerful of holy men.

It was these thoughts that kept Grayfeather's mind occupied as he crawled through the grass on his belly like
just another of the local serpents. These, and his plans for
Emma Deerborne's future.

The time for her death had come.

Knowing such a thing was another of the many arts
that Grayfeather had learned. Without taking such pains
to become familiar with his prey, Grayfeather knew he
would stop being a hunter and start walking the path of
the murderer. Even though this was a job that needed to
be done, he couldn't do it unless he was sure he could
strike a true blow and deliver Emma Deerborne into the
spirit world with as little pain and fear as possible.

She couldn't be stricken by something as crude as a
bullet while running away.

She couldn't have her throat sliced while her eyes were
open wide enough to see it coming.

She would be put down cleanly and quickly or she
would not be harmed at all.

This was what none of Grayfeather's partners could
never understand. And so, it was for the best that he complete his hunt without them. Emma Deerborne would be
ushered with a kind hand into the next life.

As for those who would stand in Grayfeather's way . . .
they would be removed from his path any way possible.

The hunt must continue.

THIRTY-FIVE

The night was cold.

Dinner was terrible. Warm strips of jerked beef, some beans, and muddy coffee.

"Sorry about all of this," Emma said after gathering up the plates and cups.

Clint shook his head. "I told you before. I want to help you and that's all there is to it. You don't have to—"

"That's not what I was talking about," Holding up the stack of dirty plates, she said, "I meant the meal. Cooking's never been a real specialty of mine."

"Oh," Clint said with a smirk. "In that case, you should be sorry." He paused to let a bubble of gas pass uncomfortably from one side of his stomach to another. "Very sorry."

"I heard some running water nearby, so I'll just wash these for you and refill our canteens."

"Don't worry about that," Clint said as he got to his feet. "At least not until morning."

Emma paused for a second with the canteens and dishes in hand before she started walking in the same direction again. "It's no trouble at all. Actually, I don't mind doing a little work. It'd make me feel as though I'm pulling at least some of my own weight around here."

Not wanting to alarm her, Clint tried to think of a delicate way to talk to her, but instead opted for the honest route. "It's not that I don't want you to do anything. But the safest place for you to be is right here ... with me. I mean, Grayfeather is still out there, after all."

His point made, Clint got up to take some of the things from Emma's hands. She handed over the dishes and then set the canteens onto the ground, shrugging her shoulders and turning away from him.

Clint set the things down on the ground behind him. A cool breeze churned the wind through Emma's dark hair, causing her to wrap her arms around herself in a gesture that had become somewhat endearing in Clint's mind. It made the woman look fragile and inviting at the same time, and although he couldn't quite pin down where the feelings were coming from, he couldn't deny that something inside him had been stirring at the sight of her.

He came up behind her and slipped his arms around Emma's midsection, clasping his hands at her waist and holding her close. The gesture was a way to test the waters with her, so Clint waited to see if the woman would struggle or try to pull away. But she did nothing of the sort. Instead, she leaned her head back onto his shoulder and let out a slow, contented sigh.

"You seem awful nervous," Clint said.

Emma's lips curled into a subtle smile. "I guess being hunted by a pack of killers will do that to you."

"Actually, you seem more nervous around me. I want you to know that I would never dream of trying to take Darryl's place."

She shrugged within his embrace, her shoulders moving easily within Clint's arms. "Darryl was a friend, but he was more of a guide than anything else. We shared a bed sometimes. That's about it." Drawing herself into an even smaller bundle, Emma turned around so she could look

up into Clint's face as her arms slipped around his waist.
"I have been a bit nervous, though."

"About what?"

She lowered her eyes for a second and then looked back
up to catch and hold Clint's gaze. "About you. Most of
the men that know about me are too scared to do much
more than say a word or two before they get away as fast
as they can. Darryl was different, but I think we just . . .
enjoyed each other for a while. Deep down inside . . . I
could tell he was scared of me too."

"Sorry to disappoint you," Clint said as he brushed
away a few strands of hair from Emma's face. "But I
don't believe in curses. In fact, I don't believe there's
anything you could do to make me see you as something
besides what you are."

Blushing, Emma asked, "And what's that?"

"A strong, honest, beautiful woman who's making the
best out of a very bad, very strange situation."

"Nobody's ever said anything like that to me before."

"It sounds like nobody's really given you much of a
chance. Besides, you've been a little busy lately. Being
hunted by a pack of killers will do that to you."

Despite everything that had happened, Emma had to
laugh at Clint's comment. The gesture made her face light
up and her arms clasp around him just a little tighter than
before. She could feel Clint's hands on her back, rubbing
slow circles down her spine. "You make me feel so safe,"
she said. "So comfortable. Like there's nothing out there
that can harm me as long as I stay close to you."

"There's not a lot of places for Grayfeather to hide
around here. And if he gets too close, we'll know about
it long before he can do anything. But that doesn't mean
you should wander off too far."

"I wouldn't dream of it," Emma said. Now her hands
were tugging at Clint's shirt, pulling it free from where it
was tucked into his pants so she could slip her hands

beneath the material and onto the skin of his back. "I want to stay close to you for as long as I can."

Clint's blood started racing through his body, his muscles tensing in anticipation wherever Emma's fingers were about to touch him. He felt as though she made his skin hot in every spot their bare skin met. Now that this moment was here, he realized that he'd been waiting for it ever since he'd gotten to know the woman who'd put herself in his care.

Every one of Emma's movements was fueled by inner confidence. Although she'd been afraid of the dangers in her life, that confidence had kept her from caving in to them. And it was that confidence that had made her so attractive in Clint's eyes.

"You don't have to do this, Emma," Clint said. "I'll take you to where you need to go no matter what."

"I know. But I need to stay close to you, don't I?" She tugged at Clint's jeans until they came open. Her leg rubbed against his thigh. "We should stay close tonight."

Clint started pulling Emma's skirt up until his hand could get beneath her slip. "Yes indeed. Very close."

THIRTY-SIX

So many times Clint and Emma had gotten close to each other, but neither one of them had pressed any further. For whatever reason, one or both of them had pulled away and tried not to think too much about what it was they truly wanted from each other. Now, as their lips finally met, they could feel an intense heat radiating from their bodies, pushing them together as their desires were unleashed.

Emma lifted one leg to wrap it around Clint's waist, moaning softly as she felt his hand pull her skirts up around her hips. She tore the shirt off his back with a force that surprised even herself, the muscles in her body responding to the pleasure of his touch.

When Clint's fingers touched the inside of her thigh, Emma let out a throaty moan while tossing her head back. She could feel the juices pumping between her legs, dripping down her skin. Feeling Clint's touch upon her exposed vagina, Emma thought she might climax right then and there. Already, small currents of pleasure rippled through her skin and caught the breath in the back of her throat.

At first, Clint had been trying to restrain himself so he

150

could take his time with her and make the moments last as long as possible. But he couldn't restrain him any longer, he realized. Not with her body so tight against him in the very moment he'd been anticipating for what felt like a small eternity.

Sliding his hand between her legs, Clint felt the hot slickness of Emma's vagina. The thin, delicate lips between her legs parted easily for him, allowing his fingers to slip inside and then tighten around him immediately.

When Clint pressed his thumb against the swollen nub of her clit, he was amazed at the strength with which Emma held on to him. Her arms clenched around his neck as she leaned back, a shuddering cry rolling out of her and into the cool night air.

Emma's leg clenched around his waist as Clint slid his fingers in and out of her. Finally, he felt her body turn rigid as she suppressed a cry of ecstasy by biting down on her lower lip. Once she'd regained control of herself, she steadied her footing and took a step back and worked Clint's jeans down around his ankles.

Kneeling before him, Emma parted her lips and ran her mouth along the side of his rigid cock. Her tongue came out just enough to tease his flesh as her hands reached around to pull him closer. After looking up into his face, she smiled widely, opened her mouth wide, and swallowed his penis whole, devouring him all the way down to its base.

Now it was Clint's turn to lose himself in the intense pleasure he was being given. While he slipped his fingers through Emma's dark, silky hair, he felt her head bobbing back and forth in a strong, steady rhythm. She opened her lips just a bit while taking him inside her mouth, only to tighten them when sliding him out. All the while, her tongue was circling his shaft, tasting every inch of him until his knees started to buckle.

The feeling was incredible. Looking up while Emma

sucked him, Clint swore the stars were circling overhead in a giant whirl of light and darkness. When he looked down again, Emma was grinning broadly, her hands sliding up over his chest as she climbed to her feet.

They took a few moments to undress each other. Clint pulled the dress over Emma's head and laid it down on the ground like a picnic blanket. The sweat on her body pasted the slip to her skin, outlining every slender curve. Feeling his eyes upon her, Emma ran her hands along her own body. Her nipples became hard as she touched her breasts with probing fingertips.

The sight of her brought a warm wave of pleasure to Clint's skin. His blood pumped through him a little faster, and when he reached out to remove the slip, instead he tore it away from her body. Emma's excited moan mingled with the sound of the thin material being ripped away in two pieces.

For a second, Emma stood in front of him with her arms resting lightly across her breasts. Then, watching Clint's eyes move over her body, she let her arms fall away and reach out for him.

Clint stepped forward, allowing her to explore his chest with fingers that were damp with her own perspiration. She rubbed every muscle and touched every inch of him, working her way down until she could strip away every last shred of clothing. Then, grabbing hold of his hands, she brought him down to the ground at her side.

They reclined on her dress, showering each other with gentle kisses for a while, their hands slowly moving up and down over each other's body. Before too long, Emma reached between Clint's legs and gently rubbed his penis, massaging it until it was thick and hard in her grasp.

Draping one leg over his side, Emma moved the tip of his cock along the inside of her thighs and then along the warm moistness between them. With a shift of his hips, he slid inside. Emma gasped once and gripped him by the shoulders, her body twitching as little jolts of pleasure crackled just beneath the surface of her flesh.

For a few seconds, neither one of them moved a muscle. Instead, they looked across at each other, savoring the moment until they couldn't wait another second.

Slowly, Clint moved back and forth, in and out of her, enjoying the tightness of her body clenching around his. The heat of her flesh and the smooth, slippery dampness that only became wetter with every stroke.

As much as Clint wanted to grab hold of her and indulge himself completely, he wasn't so willing to rush forward any faster than he had to. He wanted to make every moment last. He wanted to savor every texture of Emma's smooth body and every contented sound that came from her lips.

She must have been thinking the same thing, because Emma chose that moment to force herself to remain still before slipping away from him. Without saying a word, she pushed Clint onto his back and straddled his hips, being careful not to allow him to slip inside.

Smiling down at him, she worked her hands over his body, massaging his muscles while his heart thumped wildly inside his chest. Both of their bodies ached for more of the carnal pleasures they'd already experienced, but they also knew the longer they put it off, the better it would be once they finally gave in to the desires raging through them.

THIRTY-SEVEN

Grayfeather had been crawling like a predatory cat for so long that he almost had forgotten about walking upright. His motions had taken on the sinewy feline qualities that had allowed him to slide soundlessly through the night. Once the sun had completely disappeared, it wasn't hard at all to spot the campfire in the distance, even though it wasn't much more than a glinting beacon on the horizon.

Before too long, he could see the source of the column of smoke that he'd been crawling toward. His nose picked up hints of a meal. Less than an hour later, his ears pricked up at the sound of voices grunting like animals.

The Sioux knew well enough what was going on. Obviously, the woman was working her curse into Clint Adams just to make sure that he fell like all the others before him. Once again, Grayfeather had to wonder why the woman would do such a thing to the men that tried to help her.

Perhaps she was like the tricksters of his people's legends. Spirits like the coyote would inflict their havoc simply because it was in their power to do so. They caused trouble because it was just their nature. They were put on this land to undo what had been made.

They were chaos incarnate . . . nothing more. Nothing less.

Centering himself back on the task at hand, Grayfeather shook away the tribal tales from his mind and continued his stealthy approach to the camp Adams had made. As he got closer, he could see fleeting glimpses of the gun-fighter and the woman.

What he saw was not a lot more than silhouettes, but he knew that they were pleasuring each other. He could tell by the wanton cries of the woman and the way the shape of their bodies entwined while standing near the flames.

The hunter within the Sioux lurched forward, salivating at the easy target presenting itself to him like a wounded animal baring its neck. Both of them were naked and vul-nerable and soon enough, they would be even more vul-nerable.

Reflexively, Grayfeather stopped where he was. The balls of his feet were pressed against the ground and one hand was in the air in front of him, poised before taking the next step. It was difficult to push the hunter down, but the man knew better than to strike so quickly at such an easy target.

If it had been anyone else up there, rutting like animals, Grayfeather would have pounced without a second's hes-itation. In fact, he'd done that very recently when the curse had taken its last victim.

But this wasn't just any man that had taken Emma Deerborne under his protection. This was Clint Adams. A gunfighter, yes, but a skilled one nonetheless. Despite the lack of true respect Grayfeather had for any gunfighter, he had to acknowledge that Adams was a superior foe.

Besides the stories Grayfeather had heard about the man, the Sioux now had his own experiences to draw from. After engaging Adams in a trial by combat, he had to admit that the gunfighter possessed a great amount of skill.

Adams would not allow his defenses to be lowered so completely unless he had made other preparations. Grayfeather found it hard to believe that a man like Adams, a true warrior, would come this far only to allow himself to be distracted in such an open area.

Such a careless man would never have been able to walk away from hand-to-hand combat with Grayfeather. Especially when he knew he was being followed, knew he was being hunted, by another warrior like himself.

No . . . a man like Clint Adams would not be taken by surprise so easily. If he was allowing himself to be distracted by the woman, then there must surely be some other defense. . . .

And then, Grayfeather saw them.

Secreted in the grass directly ahead of him, and blending almost seamlessly into the environment, was the brittle thicket of branches that Grayfeather had almost walked right into without thinking. The twigs could very well have fallen to the ground and been blown into place by the wind, but that possibility faded quickly away when the Sioux strained his eyes to peer a bit further into the darkness.

Testing the ground with his fingers while being careful not to put any weight on them, he felt for where the branches were placed. It was obvious that they were strewn about to cover an area that was big enough that Grayfeather wouldn't have been able to clear it even if he tried leaping over it.

He could see the occasional twig poking up from the grass, spaced just close enough together that he couldn't crawl through them either without the danger of snapping several of them in the process. He knew just how loud that snapping would be in an open area like this. He knew

because he'd trained to avoid making such noises for
years.

No, those weren't blown in place by the wind.

They'd been set there as an alarm. Although crude, the
system was elegant enough for Grayfeather to give Adams
a little more respect. It didn't take more than a few
minutes of circling the campsite for Grayfeather to realize
that the branches did indeed form a ring around the perimeter.

Laying with his body pressed against the cool, familiar
soil, the Sioux inched away from the branches while his
mind swam with the possibilities of what other traps could
be waiting for him closer to that crackling fire.

There could be animal traps, snares, or nothing at all.
Either way, it was Adams who got what he wanted by
forcing Grayfeather to halt his advance if only for the
moment.

He could still hear the sounds of the couple enjoying
each other as he backed away from the camp. Searching
for a spot where he could lie and wait in cover, Grayfeather was unable to find much of anything for almost
half an hour. By the time he did, he'd been forced to
retread nearly a hundred yards.

Another small victory for Adams.

So be it, Grayfeather thought. The gunfighter would
have to leave eventually. And when he did . . . the hunt
would go on.

THIRTY-EIGHT

Clint thought he would be satisfied simply lying with Emma there under the stars. Their naked forms reclined together as their hands played over each other's skin. Her slender hips and firm buttocks felt like an exquisite sculpture beneath his fingers. She made a sound close to a purr whenever he massaged her pert breasts. That purr turned into a sharp groan and her eyes snapped open when he leaned down to gently close his teeth around her nipples.

That jolt of energy was enough to ignite the fires that had been smoldering inside Emma over the last several minutes. She crawled on her hands and knees until she sat on top of him, looking down into Clint's eyes with naked lust.

She ground her slick pussy against his cock, not allowing it to penetrate her body. Savoring the tortured expression on Clint's face, Emma crawled off him and made her way around his body until her face was directly over his. After showering him with a few intense kisses, she slithered over Clint's body, running her tongue over his lips, down his neck, across his chest, and then along the inside of his thighs. Emma settled her pussy over Clint's

158

mouth, lowering it onto his waiting tongue while sucking on his cock.

Clint buried his tongue inside her and thrust his face between her legs for only a short while. Grabbing her tight little ass, he slapped her playfully on the rump and slid back beneath her. He stopped once Emma was right where he wanted her; straddling his hips with her back to him.

His cock was so hard that it took no more than a slight shift for him to slip it inside her pussy. Keeping ahold of her hips, Clint pushed into her with one solid thrust. She was so wet that he was able to bury his cock all the way inside her creamy depths, causing Emma to arch her back and groan loudly with pleasure.

Emma leaned forward and held onto Clint's legs. Gathering her feet beneath her so that she was squatting down on top of him, she rode up and down on his thick column of flesh, impaling herself again and again as her groans became louder and louder.

Pumping in time to her motions, Clint thrust his cock deep in between Emma's legs. Every time their hips met, a wave of sensation swept through his body, each one more powerful than the one that had come before. As they moved together, Clint watched the way Emma's body tensed with the effort of their lovemaking.

The muscles in her back were tight and well defined in the flickering light. Beads of sweat rolled down the curve of her spine as her shoulders relaxed and tensed and her entire body rose and fell on top of him. At one point, she straightened her back and slid her fingers through her hair, creating a beautiful line down the middle of her frame.

Clint sat up just enough so that he could reach around and cup her breasts from behind. The moment his fingers closed around her soft flesh, Emma put her hands on top of his, pressing him harder to herself. She leaned back so that her back was almost resting on his chest, her legs spread wide so he could continue to pump inside her.

Holding that position nearly sapped all of Emma's strength, but it allowed Clint to rub against a spot inside her that brought her to her next trembling orgasm. The pleasure was so intense that it started her entire body shaking. The scream that she wanted to let out was stuck inside her, allowing no more than a strained groan to be heard.

Clint took hold of her and rolled Emma onto the ground. Her face was wet with perspiration, but she urged him to keep going with wide, pleading eyes. Settling in between her thighs, Clint set one of Emma's legs on his shoulder before guiding himself into her once again.

Almost too spent to move, Emma lay on her back with her arms stretched out over her head, shifting her hips when she could. The moment Clint buried his cock inside her, she clenched her eyes shut and let out a shuddering cry. He slid all the way inside her, grinding against her body before sliding back out again. Every time he repeated the motion, he brought her close to yet another climax. His hands slid down her hips and up her body, coming to a rest on her breasts, where they stayed as he pumped faster and faster.

Clint couldn't get enough of Emma's body. Her tight little pussy held onto him as though she didn't want to let go. The smell of her sex made Clint's blood pump harder through his veins. He could feel her nipples growing even harder beneath the palms of his hands.

Just when Emma tensed around him for the third time, Clint felt his own body building toward its inevitable explosion. The sensation pulsed inside him, growing with every thrust, building up even faster as Emma started squealing with delight.

Finally, Clint reached his climax and was holding onto Emma with every ounce of strength his body could muster.

When the waves had worked their way through his system, Clint reluctantly started to move away.

"Don't go," Emma whispered. "Stay right where you are. Just for a little while."

Clint did just that. He shifted so that they were on their sides, but still joined. They lay there, entwined together, until Emma drifted off into a deep contented sleep.

Clint managed to slip out of her arms less than twenty minutes later. After moving Emma into a more comfortable position and covering her with a blanket, he dressed and stood watch over the camp.

Even with the makeshift alarms set up around the perimeter, he knew he shouldn't have let his guard down for so long. But as he thought back to what they'd just done, it was hard for him to feel bad about his pleasant diversion.

But that couldn't happen again, he knew. Not tonight anyway. He'd been lucky that Grayfeather hadn't snuck up on them while they were both indisposed. Trying to ignore the part of his brain that berated him for his bad timing, Clint focused on all the sounds around him.

He listened to every chirp. Every rustle. Every gust.

All the while, he waited for the sound of Grayfeather's approach. Just one snap of those branches would be enough to set him off. And until he heard it, he wouldn't sleep a single wink.

THIRTY-NINE

Luck wasn't something that just happened to anybody.

Luck was a skill.

It was something that could be learned and cultivated the same way others might learn to read or ply their trade. It was something that might happen accidentally every once in a while, but it was never consistent unless a man knew how to nurture it so that it would come back and stay with him no matter where he went or what he did.

Douglas Rhyne was such a man.

He was familiar with his own kind of luck, and knew how to squeeze every last bit out of him when he needed it the most. And it had taken every drop of his luck, as well as everything he had in reserve, to track down where Clint Adams had gone with that bitch Emma Deerborne.

Rhyne knew which way the woman wanted to go, and luckily, there wasn't much on that trail to cover any tracks. Being a tracker of men for most of his life, Rhyne was able to catch his first sight of them earlier in the day. Actually, he'd caught the sound of gunfire and then caught sight of Adams scuffling with the Injun.

Now that had been one hell of a show.

Once Rhyne realized what was happening and who was

doing the fighting, he'd sat right back to enjoy the spectacle. Despite everything he knew about Clint Adams, he never thought The Gunsmith would be able to stand up to someone as fast with a blade as Grayfeather. Of course, after Adams was able to draw his gun, Rhyne was certain the Injun was going to catch some lead.

He couldn't believe his eyes when not one, but both men managed to get away from the brawl alive. In fact, that boosted Rhyne's respect for both of them considerably. However, that wouldn't be enough to save their lives when the chips started to fall.

The simple fact was that Rhyne was in this to secure his livelihood. The money he was set to make would be enough to see him through for the next couple years, and for that he would put down both Adams and Grayfeather even if he had to pick them off from a distance.

Honor didn't mean much to a professional. That stuff was for fools and soldiers. And since neither of those two groups had many rich men in them, Rhyne was perfectly happy with who he was.

Once Grayfeather crept away, Rhyne was able to follow Adams all the way to his campsite. Since he knew how the Injun thought, he put plenty of distance between himself and Adams so he wouldn't run into Grayfeather until he was ready to meet up with the red man on his own terms.

It would be too risky to make a fire for himself, since that would only attract unwanted attention. For now, Rhyne was content to sleep in the dark until the first light of dawn woke him up. That way, when he showed his face again, it would be a surprise to both Adams and Grayfeather.

Just thinking about all the ways he could take advantage of a surprise like that brought a smile to Rhyne's face. He was filled with confidence that night. After all, if he could actually sneak up on the likes of those two, he deserved every bit of the money he'd be getting.

Tomorrow would be the day. Rhyne could feel the luck charging through his veins.

Good for him.

Bad for everyone else.

FORTY

Clint slept about as well as a statue that had been carved with its eyes open. Throughout the entire night, he could feel unconsciousness creeping up on him and drawing his entire body to the ground, where he could stretch out and get even just a couple minutes of rest.

But all the while, he knew that if he closed his eyes, he wouldn't open them until the sun was shining on his face. So instead of allowing himself to do what he so badly needed to do, he acted as though he didn't even possess eyelids.

He blinked only when necessary. He kept watch on the quiet, unmoving night and forgot what the word "sleep" even meant. The few times he was unable to fight back the occasional nap, his eyes still remained open and he was awake again within seconds.

Knowing that he'd managed to sneak in a few winks here and there, Clint checked on Emma at the first sign of dawn just to make sure that she hadn't been harmed during one of his momentary lapses.

The only injuries she'd suffered were a few scrapes on her knees, which had actually come from their activities from the night before. Clint was about to wake her so

they could get a start on the day's travel, but he decided
to let her sleep for a few minutes longer while he packed
up their things. In a way, he got a small bit of relief
hearing the slow rhythm of Emma's breathing. It was almost as though he was resting vicariously through her,
which was all the rest he would allow himself until they
reached safer ground.

Clint was gathering up the few things that lay near the
campfire when he heard a sound that he'd been waiting
for the entire night. It wasn't much. Just the scraping of
a few of the dry branches against the ground. The noise
was enough to catch Clint's ear, which had been straining
to hear something like that over the last several hours. He
knew it couldn't have come from the wind, so that left
only one other possibility.

Someone was moving toward the campsite, and was
doing it so well that he'd almost slipped in beneath even
Clint's straining senses.

Freezing in the middle of what he'd been doing, Clint
was careful not to make another sound until he could pin-
point the exact direction the new arrival was coming from.
He crouched near the charred remains of the fire like
something that had been planted there until he heard the
sound of movement one more time.

It came from the edge of the campsite on the side closest to where Emma was lying. He could hear it clearly
now, and there was something else besides the first sound
that was coming through as well. Stepping over Emma's
resting form, Clint strained his eyes to see any trace of
motion in the area where the noise was coming from. But
all he could see was the knee-length grass laced with the
branches that he'd put there himself.

No matter how quiet any man could be, he wouldn't
have been able to keep the grass from parting beneath his
weight. And someone the size of Grayfeather would have

created a large dent in the filmy green haze created by the slowly waving blades of grass.

But even though he couldn't see what was moving, Clint could still hear it. Making sure to keep the back of one heel touching Emma's body so he could keep track of her whereabouts, Clint crouched down to get a better look at the edge of the small clearing as the rustling sound drew closer . . .

. . . and closer . . .

There still wasn't much to see, and the sound itself was nothing more than a whisper on top of the wind. Clint was just about to dismiss his concerns as the result of a sleepless night when he heard another sound that made the hairs on the back of his neck stand on end.

Hissing . . . followed by a distinct rattle.

Clint froze once again. This time, however, he did so because he knew what was coming mere seconds before the rattler poked its head out from the grass. The snake's wide, leathery face emerged from the surrounding field of green on a direct course for Emma's face. It stopped after no less than a foot and a half of it was in the shorter grass of the campsite.

The snake's body was about as thick as Emma's fore-arm, and the markings on its skin told Clint that it was a diamondback rattler, one of the deadliest of its kind. Test-ing the air with a flickering tongue, the snake moved its head back and forth as more of its body kept pouring out from the grass.

There were less than two feet separating Clint from the rattler by the time the snake's tail came into view. The serpent's rattle had the look of decayed bone, and shook erratically at the end of its body. Sensing Clint's presence, the snake coiled its body defensively, every muscle along its four-foot length tensing to strike.

Clint knew he had to stay absolutely still so as not to provoke the deadly creature. A bite from a diamondback would easily be enough to kill him. Even a small dose of its venom could cause whatever part of him it sank its fangs into to swell up and rot away after a long and painful ordeal.

He could simply try to get it to slither off in another direction if not for the fact that it was still within striking distance of Emma. Suddenly, Clint wondered offhandedly if whoever had cursed her had had poisonous snakes in mind at the time.

The snake turned its head to one side and then wavered back toward Clint, before lying flat on the ground and sliding another couple of inches closer to his boot. Although it knew Clint was there, the rattler seemed more interested in the bigger target presented by the smooth, unsuspecting flesh of the woman lying in front of it.

Following the snake with his eyes, Clint shifted his weight onto his back leg while moving his hand toward his Colt. In one swift motion, he snapped out his front leg, catching the rattler just beneath its midsection and launching it into the air.

Confused and surprised, the snake twisted in midair with its fangs extended, venom dripping in anticipation. Its body flexed forward and its mouth opened wide just as a single bullet exploded through the air to blow off the top of its fist-sized head.

Behind him, Emma jolted awake with a yelp. That yelp became a full-fledged scream when she caught sight of the thick, scaly body that landed on the ground less than a foot in front of her.

Clint dropped the Colt back into its holster and reached down to pick up the twitching snake's body. The rattler convulsed reflexively as if to take a bite at him, even though it only had part of its lower jaw remaining.

Holding the diamondback in the air for a second, Clint said, "There's a lot of folks who wouldn't mind keeping the tail of one of these for a keepsake, you know."

Jumping to her feet, Emma managed to compose herself enough to fight back the urge to run away from the gruesome sight. "Well, I'm not one of them. Get that horrible thing away from me."

Clint turned to toss it into the grass on the other side of the campsite. The rattler left his hand and was sailing through the air before Clint turned around to see exactly where it landed. Instead of the thump he expected to hear once the snake hit the ground, he heard the snap of several dry branches breaking and a sharp slap.

Every instinct in Clint's head sparked to life. He swiveled around and drew the Colt again in a single action, bringing the pistol to bear on whoever had walked through the branches surrounding his campsite.

Standing there, with the dead rattler hanging from one fist, was Douglas Rhyne. "Beautiful shot, Adams," he said. "Maybe there's a way around that curse after all."

FORTY-ONE

"Who the hell are you?" Clint asked without shifting his aim away from the new arrival.

The man dropped the snake and held his hands in the air. "The name's Rhyne."

"The one that worked with Grayfeather?"

"The same. I guess the little lady over there told you all about me, huh?"

Clint nodded. "She told me there were others after her besides the Indian. Since I don't recognize you, that means you must be after her and yours was the only other name she mentioned. Why don't you toss your pistol over here and we can discuss what brings you out this far."

"No need for that. I know who you are and I ain't got a wish to die. You don't have to worry about me drawing on you."

"If it's all the same to you, I'd feel a lot more comfortable if you'd hand it over just the same."

"Since you know about the red man, then you know that the rattler you bagged might not be the only snake in the grass around here. I came to you to offer my help with that other snake. If he's anywhere around here, he'll kill me first as soon as he sees me throw away my gun."

Taking a few steps back, Clint motioned for Rhyne to step forward. "I'm still a bit jumpy, so toss the weapon and come speak your piece. If Grayfeather shows up, he'll keep me plenty busy enough for you to take it back."

"Fair enough," Rhyne said after pondering for a second or two. Being careful to hold the gun using only his thumb and forefinger, he lifted it from his holster and tossed it against the stones surrounding the black pile of twigs that had been the campfire.

"Don't trust him," Emma said from directly behind Clint. "He killed Darryl and he'll kill us as soon as he gets the chance."

Holstering the Colt, Clint replied, "Oh, I don't trust him. But he knows I can outdraw him, so that should keep him in check for a minute or two." Stepping up near the fire, Clint came to a stop with one boot resting squarely on Rhyne's pistol. "Now what is it you wanted to say?"

"Just a friendly warning is all. That one there," Rhyne said while pointing to Emma, "she's a black widow. Just like them spiders that kills after they mate—"

"I know what a black widow is. Just get to the point."

"Then you should also know that every one of them that tried to help her either got themselves killed or hurt one way or another. And the few that made it out with their skins intact ran away as soon as they saw what was comin' for them."

"Funny," Clint said. "But all I ever heard about was the firsthand accounts that say it was you and the Indian who did all the killing. That doesn't sound like much of a curse to me. It's more like good old-fashioned murder."

"Yeah? And I suppose there was nothin' that nearly reached out of that there grass and pumped you full of poison either?"

Clint shook his head and stifled a laugh. "In case you forgot . . . this is Texas. And Texas is full of rattlesnakes.

Some just happen to walk on their bellies, while others walk on two legs like yourself."

"I'm doing you a service by telling you that this here bitch is bad luck. The men that traveled with her didn't all get shot. Some fell and broke their necks. Others got stung by scorpions or the like. And one got trampled by his own horse. That ain't coincidence, Adams. That's bad luck, pure and simple."

Clint spotted Emma walking around him from the corner of his eye. She stood on the edge of his vision and put her hands on his elbow.

"It's true," she said softly. "I told you . . . that's why we need to get to Oklahoma."

Knowing better than to take his eyes away from a killer like Rhyne for even a second, Clint held himself steady as a rock. A cold, uneasy feeling was working its way up along his spine when he said, "Get the rope from my saddle, Emma. We're taking this man to the law in the next town we come to."

Rhyne didn't even react to those words. Instead, he simply shrugged and shook his head. "You've spent a lot of time with her, Adams. I thought you might like to know what happens to them that gets too close."

"What did you think you'd gain by coming here?" Clint asked. "Did you figure I'd thank you for the warning, give you a pat on the back, and send you on your way? Maybe toss in a little reward as a thank-you?"

"Nah," Rhyne said. "I told you that I just wanted to talk for a while, which is exactly what I've done."

Clint could hear Emma working on getting the rope from where the horses were tied behind him. Suddenly, the wind that had been tossing the grass from side to side died off as though it had been choked off from the source. When that happened, there was still a sound that lingered for no more than half a second before dying off as well.

That second sound didn't sit right in Clint's mind. In

fact, it struck him so much that he shifted his eyes away from Rhyne to take a look at what might have caused it. The first thing he saw was a clear spot in the middle of the taller grass that he swore hadn't been there before.

Just as his instincts were beginning to send flickers of warning throughout his mind, Clint saw a shape spring out from the grass with much of the same fluidity as the rattler, except nearly twice as fast. The figure reared up and flew outward amid the crackle of snapping branches that had remained undisturbed until this moment when Grayfeather had worked his way almost right up to Emma's side.

Clint felt urgency pump through his body, causing him to duck reflexively as the Sioux lashed out with a tomahawk aimed for his jugular. While barely dodging the blow, Clint threw himself toward Emma and wrapped his arms around her waist, taking her down with him as he landed heavily on the ground near Eclipse's legs.

"Finally," Rhyne shouted as he dove for his gun. "I thought you'd never show up."

FORTY-TWO

Grayfeather's body was a constant flow of motion. He was just as comfortable leaping through the air as he was landing on his feet, and the moment he'd followed through with his first strike, he was pulling the tomahawk back to take another swipe at his target. Glaring around with cold, focused eyes, the Sioux took in every last detail around him in the space of a heartbeat. By the time he blinked again, he'd already assessed his situation and planned his next attack.

In stark contrast to the Sioux's fluid movements, Rhyne all but threw himself into the dirt, scrambling to get ahold of his gun like he was in the middle of a game of hot potato. Despite his lack of grace, he still managed to get his weapon in hand and ready to fire without missing more than a beat or two.

Clint didn't have to take in the scene to know what was going on. Hard-earned instincts along with an entire night of memorizing every last inch of the campsite gave him the ability to move with his eyes closed if necessary while guessing where the other men would go and what they would do.

"Get out of here," Clint said to Emma. "Don't worry about me, just go!"

Although she was about to protest, Emma saw the hulking form of Grayfeather bearing down on Clint like the shadow of death itself. That was more than enough to get her to forget any thoughts she might have had of staying at the campsite. Instead, she leapt to her feet and jumped onto the back of her horse, digging her heels into its side to race away from the camp.

Clint listened to the pounding of hooves against the earth just long enough to be satisfied that Emma was out of harm's way. He twisted his body to roll onto his back, bringing his arms up to guard his face just as Grayfeather's fists came crashing down toward him.

The Sioux was on him so fast that he seemed to have been shot out of a cannon. His face was covered with numerous little cuts, a few of which were still dripping blood. When his arms were stopped in mid-strike by Clint's hasty block, the impact was enough to rattle both men down to the bone.

"Still sharp after a night on your feet, eh?" Grayfeather said through tightly clenched teeth. "You managed to build up just enough around you to keep me at bay. Do you have any tribal blood in you?"

"No," Clint said while straining with every ounce of his might. He was barely able to keep the tomahawk from pressing into his cheek while the Sioux's other hand fought to wrap around his throat. "But I'm about to have tribal blood on me as soon as I get my hands on you."

Grayfeather started to react to the statement, but winced suddenly in pain as Clint's knee smashed into his lower ribs. The blow sent shards of pain through the Indian's body, and broke his concentration just long enough for Clint to shift his weight beneath him and throw Grayfeather onto the ground.

Rolling toward the circle of stones in the middle of

camp, Clint came to a stop with his feet beneath him and picked himself up off the ground. The first thing he looked for was Rhyne's gun. Seeing it wasn't there, he shifted to quickly take a glance around him, hoping to catch sight of the other man before . . .

First came the snap of a hammer being cocked back. Hearing that, Clint ducked low and stepped back. Next, there was a gunshot, which was followed quickly by another.

One bullet whipped through the air near Clint, but the second wasn't even close. Figuring that even a poor shot would have done a better job than that, Clint looked toward the source of the gunfire to see what had pulled Rhyne so far off target.

The answer was simple. Rhyne had more than one target.

Although Clint didn't believe his eyes at first, it was plain to see that Rhyne had been aiming that second shot at Grayfeather. Clint wasn't one to question any opening he could get in a fight, and his hand flashed for the Colt at his side. He plucked the weapon from its holster and brought it up in the same heartbeat. Before he could pull the trigger, however, he felt a stabbing pain in his right hand that traveled all the way up through his wrist.

Looking down, Clint saw one of the smooth rocks from the ring around the campfire falling to the ground and landing near his right boot. That had been what had struck him, and it had been thrown by the man who decided to ignore Rhyne altogether and charge Clint instead.

Grayfeather held the tomahawk down low near his leg while charging forward. Without taking his eyes from Clint, he scooped up another rock from the campfire and tossed it to the side as if he was skipping it across a lake. This time, it whipped through the air to smack heavily against Rhyne's temple, dropping the gunman like a sack of manure.

The Colt began slipping through Clint's numb fingers, his hand in too much pain to respond to any of his mental commands. Rather than fight against his own body, Clint let the pistol drop and swung his left arm in a tight semicircle to knock aside the incoming tomahawk. He struck Grayfeather on the wrist while turning his head to one side as the tomahawk passed within an inch of his nose.

Not one single emotion registered on the Sioux's face. There was no anger. No fear. Not even frustration. There were simply the cold, unfeeling dead man's eyes that stared at Clint and followed him no matter which way he twisted or which direction he dodged.

"It's too late for you, Clint Adams," Grayfeather said. "You've got too much of her curse in you now. It's a disease. You'll only spread it if I let you live."

Instead of pulling back to take another swing, Grayfeather leaned all his weight onto Clint and pushed the tomahawk closer against his flesh.

Clint could feel the Indian's breath as he spoke. He could also see the perfect, razor edge of the tomahawk's stone head. He knew if he let up just a little in his struggle against the Sioux, that the tomahawk would be driven right through his neck. At this point, any wrong move could put him at Grayfeather's mercy.

Unfortunately, Clint knew damn well the Indian didn't have any mercy.

FORTY-THREE

Although Clint was able to keep the tomahawk from scraping against his neck, he knew his strength wouldn't hold out forever. Besides, Grayfeather was on top of him, which gave the Indian the advantage since gravity would be working with him.

"The way . . . I see it," Clint said while fighting to keep from getting his head cut from his shoulders, "Emma's not . . . the cursed one . . ."

Leaning down to press his weight against the tomahawk's handle, Grayfeather said, "Really? She seems to have put you in this rather unfortunate position."

"She . . . didn't do any . . . of this." Straining until his face turned red with the effort, Clint managed to push the tomahawk half an inch away from him. "You did this . . . *you're* the curse."

"Maybe so," Grayfeather replied. "But either way, it will be lifted once she is dead."

Pushing up one last time, Clint waited until he'd saved up enough strength in the rest of his body to twist himself to the right while guiding the tomahawk to the left as it dropped downward. The stone blade missed his throat, but still shredded off several layers of Clint's skin and gouged a piece from his shoulder as well.

Clint kept one hand on the tomahawk so that he knew where it was as he wrenched Grayfeather off balance and pitched him to the ground. Thinking back to the last time they'd fought, Clint remembered a weak spot on the Indian that he'd put there himself.

When Grayfeather turned to try and pull his tomahawk from Clint's grasp, he let out a pained howl as the edge of Clint's hand smashed into the tender flesh along his left side where he'd been shot the day before. Fresh blood seeped from the wound to darken the stain that had been put there by a well-placed bullet from a modified Colt.

Instead of allowing himself to get distracted by the pain, Grayfeather used it to push his body to new limits. He wrenched the tomahawk away from Clint with a savage twist of his wrist and entire upper body. Using that momentum, he bent at the waist and sent a brutal kick directly into Clint's exposed midsection.

All the air was driven from Clint's lungs with that single blow. Dark black and red blobs danced in front of his eyes, and the next breath he took felt like he'd inhaled a mouthful of broken glass. Another wave of agony followed the moment he grabbed hold of his torso and tried to move. At least one rib had been broken by the Sioux's kick. Possibly two.

Grayfeather knew that he'd delivered a powerful blow. Taking a moment to calm his breathing, he turned his back on Clint and took a step away. In the next second, he twisted around with his entire body, spinning in a lightning-fast half circle and swinging his leg out like a club.

The spinning kick caught Clint right across the jaw. It didn't do much damage, but the strike was only meant to stun the gunfighter for a few seconds. Also, it was the

Sioux's way of pressing his advantage and keeping his
opponent off guard.

Having to squint through the pain that coursed through
his body, Clint didn't see the kick coming until it had
already slammed against his face. Blood seeped into his
mouth, but compared to the grating in his ribs, the kick
to the jaw was just a minor sting. Clint noticed the smug,
victorious look on Grayfeather's face, and decided to buy
himself a few moments by playing up to the Indian's ex-
pectations.

Groaning under his breath, Clint started to get up and
then acted as though he simply didn't have the strength.
When he plopped back down to the ground, he managed
to get himself just a little bit closer to his Colt.

"You are a worthy opponent," Grayfeather said as he
walked away from Clint. Tossing his tomahawk lightly
from one hand to another, he turned and fixed Clint with
an intense stare. "If not for the bad medicine tainting your
soul, I might have let you live. But I have been sent to
perform an important task and I must put that ahead of
everything else . . . no matter how hard it might be."

Clint managed to set the pain aside for the time being.
Rather than think about the throbbing in his side or the
blood dripping from the corner of his mouth, he focused
on nothing but the Indian. Grayfeather's words fell upon
deaf ears, but those weren't what Clint cared about.

After fighting with this man, Clint had been able to get
a sense for Grayfeather's style. And although Clint might
not have been an expert in whatever techniques the Indian
was using, he'd been in enough scrapes to know what he
was doing. He also knew that he had one last chance to
pull himself out of this mess alive.

The Colt was within reach, but he wasn't completely
sure he could move faster than Grayfeather. But with precious moments dwindling away, Clint knew he was going
to have to take a gamble. However things turned out, he

would at least know for sure if there was any truth at all
to the curse that was supposedly hanging over his head.

Grayfeather stopped once he was about six paces away
from Clint. He squared his shoulders and locked his gaze
onto his target. The Indian's fingers tensed around the
tomahawk's handle while his arm slowly raised upward.

Knowing that he had to make every move count, Clint
stopped playing up his injuries and shifted another fraction of an inch closer to his Colt.

Each second seemed to take a year to pass. Neither man
took notice of anything else in the world besides what his
opponent was doing. And when Grayfeather's arm
brought the tomahawk up behind his ear, that was the
signal for both of them to make their last, desperate play.

Twisting his upper body as his arm went back, Grayfeather spun around while dropping into a low crouch. He
looked as though he was twisting his lower body into the
ground itself like a small, dying tornado. When he came
around to face Clint again, he used the momentum from
his spin to send the tomahawk whipping through the air.

The Indian's weapon spun once in the air before reaching its target, moving so fast that Clint didn't have enough
time to move more than a few muscles before the blade
was driving toward the middle of his skull.

Using every bit of speed that he'd acquired over years
of practice, Clint waited until the last moment before his
hand flashed up like a flicker of lightning and snatched
the tomahawk from the air, stopping it less than an inch
from his forehead.

For a full second, both men stood perfectly still. They
each stared at the tomahawk as though they were waiting
for it to complete its journey. When Clint blinked away
the shock in his system, he flipped the hatchet around and
sent it sailing back to its owner with a flick of his wrist.

Grayfeather might have been amazed at what he'd seen,
but he was still able to catch the tomahawk with relative

ease. Unfortunately, when he turned his eyes back to
Clint, the gunfighter had another surprise for him.

"You've got one chance to live, Grayfeather," Clint
said while staring along the barrel of the Colt, which he'd
just managed to retrieve in the time the Indian had been
distracted. "Don't waste it."

Shaking his head, Grayfeather said nothing in reply.
Instead, he cocked the tomahawk behind his ear. . . .

The Colt bucked in Clint's hand. A single piece of lead
cut through the air and drilled a messy hole through Grayfeather's skull.

The first thing to hit the dirt was the tomahawk, which
slid out of the Indian's hand. Grayfeather remained standing for a full two seconds before teetering back and finally
dropping. His head lolled to one side, locking the dead
man's eyes on Clint one last time.

FORTY-FOUR

Emma had been reluctant to leave Clint behind, but she knew she would only get in the way if she stayed at the campsite. Still, she wasn't about to go more than twenty feet or so away. Riding her own horse and leading Eclipse by the reins, she came to a stop where she could see what was happening and be ready to go back and take Clint out of there whenever it became necessary.

The fight had barely gotten under way when she saw a figure running toward her. At first, she thought it might have been Clint, but that was only wishful thinking. It didn't take long for her to realize that the man was the same one who'd shot Darryl. And before she could do anything about it, the killer had spotted her and was already aiming his gun.

"This is even better," Rhyne said as he stumbled toward Emma. "I can get ahold of you without even havin' to worry about them other two." Once he was close enough, he pointed his .44 at Emma and smiled broadly. "And you even brought a horse for me. Ain't that sweet?"

Trying to move as smoothly as she could without being noticed, Emma eased her hand toward the rifle holstered on the side of Clint's saddle. She didn't get within a foot

of the weapon before she was stopped by the sound of
Rhyne's hammer snapping back.

"Now that's not very nice," he said. "Maybe taking you
alive would be too much trouble after all, what with you
tryin' to escape the whole way. Them Injuns that want
you won't care anyway since you're cursed and all."

The smile on Rhyne's face widened when he noticed
the tears welling up in Emma's eyes. "Cursed," he spat.
"That's the biggest crock of shit I ever heard. But
money's money. I guess it don't matter how crazy the
people payin' it are."

Rhyne brought the gun up to take careful aim. Winking
once at Emma, he pulled the trigger.

The explosion was loud enough to make Emma's ears
hurt. For a moment, she knew she'd been hit and was
waiting for the pain to settle in. But then she realized there
was no pain. There was no wound. Just the ringing . . .
and someone screaming.

Opening her eyes, she saw Rhyne hunched over in front
of her, clutching a bloody stump of a hand and dropping
the blackened, twisted hunk of steel that had been his
pistol. She might not have been an expert in firearms, but
Emma knew a backfire when she saw one.

Rhyne hit the ground and rolled onto his side. Almost
instantly, his eyes widened and his screams took on a
higher pitch. He then tried to scoot backward away from
a spot in the grass, using his bloody stump and all.

Emma knew she had to do something, but didn't know
if she could get herself to use Clint's rifle on the wounded
killer. But then she saw the slender shapes darting out
from the grass toward Rhyne.

They looked like fat, leather whips darting from the
ground and hissing loudly. Soon, she could hear the rattles
and knew that Rhyne had stumbled upon the nest of di-
amondbacks that had spawned the single visitor they'd
gotten back at the campsite.

First one and then another rattler lashed out with fangs bared, latching onto Rhyne's face and arm and digging in as far as their teeth could go. Before he toppled over, a third, fourth, and fifth snake joined in the feast. By the time the sixth found its mark, Rhyne had stopped screaming.

He'd also stopped moving.

"What the hell happened here?" Clint said as he walked toward the horses with his hand pressed tightly against his side.

Emma brought the horses closer to him, making sure to give Rhyne's body a wide berth. "Let's just get out of here," she said wearily. "Right now."

FORTY-FIVE

They rode into Oklahoma a few days later. In the end, Clint watched as a tribal medicine man took Emma into a ritual that would supposedly cleanse her over the course of a few weeks.

"I guess this is good-bye," she said before handing herself over to the tribal healer. "How can I ever thank you?"

Clint kissed her gently on the cheek. "Just get yourself well. And try to stay out of trouble."

Nodding, she kissed him on the lips and followed the medicine man.

Clint hopped onto Eclipse's back and snapped the reins. The Caddos offered to feed him and give him a place to rest for the night, but Clint politely refused. All he wanted was to get back on the trail.

"I swear," Clint said once he and Eclipse were safely away from the tribe, "if I never hear about this again, it'll be too soon." Shaking his head, he muttered, "*Curses. What a load of crap.*"

Watch for

RANDOM GUNFIRE

247th novel in the exciting GUNSMITH series
from Jove

Coming in July!

J. R. ROBERTS
THE
GUNSMITH